Revenge of
the Geek

Revenge of the Geek

Piper Banks

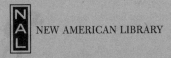

NEW AMERICAN LIBRARY

NEW AMERICAN LIBRARY
Published by New American Library,
a division of Penguin Group (USA) Inc.,
375 Hudson Street, New York, New York 10014, USA
Penguin Group (Canada), 90 Eglinton Avenue East, Suite 700, Toronto,
Ontario M4P 2Y3, Canada (a division of Pearson Penguin Canada Inc.)
Penguin Books Ltd., 80 Strand, London WC2R 0RL, England
Penguin Ireland, 25 St. Stephen's Green, Dublin 2,
Ireland (a division of Penguin Books Ltd.)
Penguin Group (Australia), 250 Camberwell Road, Camberwell,
Victoria 3124, Australia (a division of Pearson Australia Group Pty. Ltd.)
Penguin Books India Pvt. Ltd., 11 Community Centre,
Panchsheel Park, New Delhi - 110 017, India
Penguin Group (NZ), 67 Apollo Drive, Rosedale, North Shore 0632,
New Zealand (a division of Pearson New Zealand Ltd.)
Penguin Books (South Africa) (Pty.) Ltd., 24 Sturdee Avenue,
Rosebank, Johannesburg 2196, South Africa

Penguin Books Ltd., Registered Offices:
80 Strand, London WC2R 0RL, England

First published by New American Library,
a division of Penguin Group (USA) Inc.

First Printing, November 2010
1   3   5   7   9   10   8   6   4   2

REGISTERED TRADEMARK—MARCA REGISTRADA

Library of Congress Cataloging-in-Publication Data

Banks, Piper.
Revenge of the geek/Piper Banks.
p. cm.
Summary: With her boyfriend, Dex, in Maine and her friends facing their own issues, Miranda
Bloom, girl genius, befriends Nora, a shy new student, but soon Nora's relentless imitation of
Miranda threatens to ruin junior year at Geek High.
ISBN 978-0-451-23134-5
[1. High schools—Fiction. 2. Schools—Fiction. 3. Interpersonal relations—Fiction. 4.
Stepfamilies—Fiction. 5. Genius—Fiction. 6. Florida—Fiction.] I. Title.
PZ7.G2128Rev 2010
[Fic]—dc22   2010028770

Set in Bulmer MT
Designed by Elke Sigal

Printed in the United States of America

For Sam

Revenge of
the Geek

Chapter One

"Just try them on, Miranda," Hannah, my stepsister, ordered me. She sounded like an army general sending troops into battle. Except that we weren't on a battlefield. It was even worse than war—we were at the mall.

Hannah had dragged me from one end of the Orange Cove Mall to the other, stopping in nearly every store we passed. We were now in J.Crew, and I was drooping with exhaustion.

"Why bother trying them on? They're my size," I said, double-checking the tag on a pair of skinny jeans. Then I saw the price. "These jeans cost eighty dollars!"

"So?"

"Why would anyone spend eighty dollars on a pair of jeans? That's insane. I could get these at Target for twenty bucks."

Hannah looked at me with a pitying expression. "No, you couldn't. Now go try them on."

I sighed. There was no point in arguing with her. I turned toward the dressing room.

"Wait," Hannah said. She handed over a huge pile of clothes—skirts, pants, tops. It looked like she'd gotten one of everything in the store. "Try these on, too."

"What? All of these?" I asked, reeling under the weight of the clothing.

"All of them," Hannah said. She checked her watch. "And you'd better hurry. If you keep wasting time, we're never going to make the movie."

Defeated, I headed to the dressing room.

"Show me everything you try on," Hannah called after me.

The next half hour was sheer hell. I know some girls love trying on clothes and think of shopping as a hobby. I am not one of those girls. Pulling countless shirts over my head and wriggling into an endless series of pants caused me to become light-headed.

"I think I need a Coke," I complained to Hannah on one of my frequent trips out of the dressing room to model an outfit for her. "My blood sugar is low."

Hannah was unmoved. "You haven't tried on the dark-washed denim pencil skirt yet."

"Seriously, I can't try on one more thing. I'm going to pass out from hunger."

"The denim pencil skirt," Hannah ordered. "I told you: we're making over your wardrobe."

"Why does it matter? They're just clothes."

Hannah looked truly shocked. "Clothes always matter," she said. "Now go try on the denim pencil skirt!"

•

Forty minutes later we left J.Crew with bags so heavy that the thin, ropy straps felt as if they were about to cut through my fingers. I was wrung out. I mentally calculated how much money I'd spent that day— it was at least half the money I'd saved that summer working as an au pair to Amelia, a ten-year-old music prodigy. My dad had offered to chip in for new school clothes, but since he'd just bought me a car—an ugly used car, but I wasn't complaining—I felt guilty asking him for money.

Hannah seemed oddly energized after our shopping expedition. "Oh, my gosh, just think of how much better you're going to look this year," she said as we made our way toward the food court.

Hannah was so beautiful that heads were swiveling as we walked by. She had a really pretty face, set off by platinum blond hair that swished across her shoulders. She was also very thin and very petite. I always felt freakishly tall and gangly when I stood next to her, like a clumsy giraffe towering over a dainty gazelle.

"Gee, thanks," I said. I didn't think my old wardrobe was *that* bad. Maybe I wasn't a fashion plate, but my clothes were unobjectionable. Jeans, T-shirts—that sort of thing.

"No problem," Hannah said, missing my sarcasm. "I bet your friends at school won't even recognize you."

Hannah and I were the same age—we were both sixteen and going into our junior year—but we attended different high schools. Hannah went to Orange Cove High. I went to the Notting Hill Independent School for Gifted Children, which was better known as Geek High. Most of the kids at Geek High had a special talent. For example, I could solve math problems—even complex ones—in my head. Growing up, my rather unflattering nickname had been the Human Calculator. And I didn't even want to be a mathematician. I wanted to be a writer.

"I don't think skinny jeans are going to mask my true identity," I said.

"Just you wait. People will see you in a whole new light," Hannah promised.

I didn't believe that for one moment. The thing about going to Geek High was that most of the kids really did care more about their studies than what their classmates were wearing. Besides, why would I want to be seen in a different light? I had lots of friends at school. Okay, sure, I had some enemies, too—like awful Felicity Glen and her toady Morgan Simpson. Felicity had mocked me endlessly over the years for my boyish figure and boring clothes. But I was pretty sure that if she couldn't make fun of my clothes, she'd just find something else to ridicule. Like my too-large nose or my wavy hair that frizzed when it was humid. Considering that I lived in South Florida, that was pretty much all the time.

Hannah paused outside a shoe store to examine the contents of the store window.

"Can we please get something to eat? I'm starving," I complained.

"You're always starving," Hannah replied. She whipped out her pink cell phone and began scrolling through her messages.

"Emmett's here," she said.

"Here in the mall?"

Hannah nodded. "Over at the Gap. He wants to meet us for lunch." She punched a rapid succession of buttons on her phone. "I'm telling him to meet us at the food court."

"Great," I said, my heart sinking.

It wasn't that I didn't like Emmett. I did. In fact, once upon a time, I'd liked him way too much. Emmett was a year ahead of me at Geek High. He was nice, an academic superstar—his specialty was science—and absolutely gorgeous. I'd had a secret crush on him for years. But Emmett had taken one look at Hannah and become instantly smitten with my stepsister. I'd been devastated at the time, but was long over it by now. For one thing, Hannah and Emmett did make an adorable couple. And, for another, I'd fallen pretty hard myself for someone else.

Dex McConnell, boyfriend extraordinaire. He really was great. Smart, bitingly funny, and very handsome, if—like me—you happen to like redheads. Dex was also an amazing surfer and had been the star player on the Orange Cove lacrosse team. Had been, as in past tense. Four days earlier Dex had left our small town of Orange Cove to go to boarding school in Maine on a lacrosse scholarship. It was an amazing opportunity for Dex, but I missed him so much that my stomach curled over on itself whenever I thought of him.

I was pretty sure Hannah had proposed this shopping trip to distract me, and so far it had been working, mostly because my I'm-stuck-in-a-shopping-mall misery was, for the time being, drowning out my missing-Dex-so-much-it-hurts misery. But that was before I found out I was going to be hanging out with Hannah and Emmett. Nothing makes you feel more alone than playing third wheel to a happy couple.

"He's meeting us by Big Top Pizza," Hannah announced, pocketing her cell phone. "Not that I'd eat the pizza there. Gag."

"Why?"

"Tiffany's boyfriend Geoff's older brother used to work at Big Top Pizza. He said that they once had a cockroach fall into the vat of pizza sauce, and their manager wouldn't let them throw out the sauce," Hannah said. "So they kept using it on the pizzas. And, get this—when they reached the bottom of the pan of sauce, the cockroach was *missing*. So it must have ended up on one of the pizzas."

"Ewww," I said.

"I know, right? Ever since I heard that, I refuse to eat there," Hannah said.

I tried not to think of how many hundreds of slices I'd eaten at Big Top Pizza over the years. I'd always viewed a slice of their pizza as my reward for withstanding the horrors of the mall.

"Um, Hannah?"

"Yes?"

"How long have you known about the cockroach pizza?"

Hannah tossed her hair back as she considered. "I'm not sure. Maybe a year or two?"

"A *year* or *two*?"

"I think. Why does it matter?"

"Why didn't you tell me about it before? It's information I would really liked to have had," I said.

Hannah shrugged. "I don't know. It never occurred to me to tell you. Look, there's Emmett."

Emmett was standing in line at the now-notorious pizzeria. He was tall—even taller than me—with broad shoulders, blond hair, and eyes the color of the ocean. He smiled when he saw us approaching.

"Do either of you want a slice?" he asked.

"No way," Hannah and I said in unison.

"And neither do you," I added.

Emmett looked confused.

"Just trust me," I said. "Let's go to Sunshine Burger instead." I shot Hannah a sidelong look. "You don't know anyone who worked there, do you?"

"Nope," she said. "It's safe, as far as I know."

"Good," I said.

Emmett looked curious, but he just shrugged, and we all headed over to Sunshine Burger. Ten minutes later we were sitting at a table with our trays. Emmett and I had ordered exactly the same thing: a double-decker cheeseburger, large fries, soda, and a chocolate shake topped with whipped cream and a maraschino cherry. Hannah had a salad with grilled chicken and low-calorie dressing on the side. After eating three bites, she groaned and pushed back her tray.

"I'm stuffed," she said.

I had just taken an enormous bite of my double-decker, so it took me a few minutes to chew and swallow before I could respond. "How can you be stuffed on two lettuce leaves and one tiny piece of chicken?"

"Hannah always eats like a bird," Emmett said, beaming at her as though there were nothing more marvelous than the ability to survive on a few sticks and twigs.

I rolled my eyes, instantly irritated. One of the many, many things I liked about Dex was that he never minded that I had as large an appetite as he did. This was quickly followed by the now-familiar pang of sadness that thinking of Dex always caused recently. He'd been gone for only four days, and it already felt like forever. We talked every day on Skype, but it wasn't the same as feeling the warmth of his hand entwined with mine or breathing in the freshly-laundered-clothes smell of him. I wasn't going to see him in person until he was home for Thanksgiving break. How was I going to make it until then?

"Miranda?" Hannah said, interrupting my sad thoughts. "Did you hear me?"

"What? No."

"I didn't think you were listening," Hannah said accusingly. "I *said* Emmett wants to come to the movies with us. Is that okay? I know we were supposed to be having a girls' day out."

"Fine with me," I said. "Emmett can be an honorary girl for the day. As long as he doesn't mind getting pedicures with us."

But now Hannah and Emmett weren't listening to me. They were staring at each other with matching goopy expressions. I could have stood on the table and belted out a rendition of "Single Ladies (Put a Ring on It)," complete with Beyoncé's dance moves, and it still wouldn't have gotten their attention.

"You've got a stray hair," Emmett told Hannah, sweeping the offending lock out of her face and tucking it behind her ear for her.

Hannah giggled and tipped her head coquettishly. "Maybe I

should cut my hair short so it stays out of my face. I've always wondered how I'd look with a really, really short style."

"Don't do that. I like it long," Emmett said, gently pulling on one of her silver-blond locks.

"You don't think I'd look pretty with short hair?" Hannah asked.

"You'd look gorgeous no matter what," Emmett said. He took her hand and brushed his lips against her knuckles.

"Gag," I said.

Hannah and Emmett both looked at me. They seemed startled to find me sitting at the table with them.

"Seriously," I said, "this is nauseating. You're going to have to stop it now before it ruins my appetite."

"Ignore her," Hannah told Emmett. "She misses Dex, so she's feeling bitter about love."

"I'm not bitter about love," I said, stung. "I happen to be very pro-love."

"How is Dex doing? Have you talked to him?" Emmett asked.

I nodded. "Yeah, I talked to him last night. He's fine. His roommate's cool, and he said that everyone on the lacrosse team gets along."

Dex had sounded really upbeat when I talked to him. I knew he'd been nervous about starting at a new school far away from home, where he didn't know anyone. It had been too great an opportunity for him to pass up. The Brown Academy had one of the top high school lacrosse programs in the country, and a lot of the lacrosse players who went there ended up getting recruited by universities such as Princeton and Cornell. I knew it was important to him to do well at his new school, and I was glad that he was adjusting to being there. But a smaller, not-so-nice part of me had hoped that he'd be missing me too much—as much as I missed him—to settle in quite so quickly.

"Are you all ready to get back to school tomorrow?" Emmett asked.

I nodded. "Actually, I can't wait. I'm on the staff of *The Ampersand* this year." *The Ampersand* was Geek High's award-winning magazine. I'd secured a coveted writer's spot on the magazine at the end of my sophomore year. "How about you?"

"Yeah, I'm ready to get back, too. I came up with a great idea for the science fair. I'm hoping to go back to nationals this year," Emmett said. Emmett had won the state science fair every year that he had entered. His sophomore year, he'd placed second in nationals for developing a system for purifying water in developing countries. "I'm working on a new way to power cars with solar energy," he continued. "The technology has been out for a while, but no one's perfected it."

"Wow. That would be amazing," I said, impressed.

"I just need to figure out how I'm going to construct the canopy, and how the solar cells will be set up," Emmett said.

It was Hannah's turn to roll her eyes. "Only Geek High students would be looking forward to school. I wish summer vacation would last forever," she said. She checked her watch. "The movie's going to start soon. We should probably head over to the theater."

"Let me just finish my burger first," I said, taking another large bite and following it with a slurp of chocolate shake.

Hannah wrinkled her nose. "I thought you said you lost your appetite."

I shrugged. "I have to get my energy back after all that shopping," I said, popping a fry into my mouth.

Chapter Two

I parked my ugly yellow car in the student lot behind Geek High, hoping no one would see me. While I very much appreciated the car, which my dad had given me at the end of the summer, there was no getting around it: the car was truly hideous. It was short, stubby, and neon yellow, with amateurishly painted black racing stripes down the sides. Still, an ugly car was better than no car at all, and it was a nice, freeing feeling to be able to drive myself to school for the very first time.

Grabbing my backpack, I climbed out of my car and shut the door. The locks on the driver's-side door didn't work, but I didn't think there was any danger of anyone stealing it.

"Oh. My. God."

I cringed. I recognized the voice even before I turned to face Felicity Glen. She was the person I had most wanted to avoid, so it figured that she'd be the first person I'd run into.

"Is that your car?" Felicity asked, hooting with laughter.

I squared my shoulders and turned to face her. Felicity was annoyingly pretty. She was petite, with fine bones, dark brown hair, and catlike green eyes. Her full lips were curved in an evil smile as she looked from me to the yellow car and back again.

"As a matter of fact, it is," I said, trying for an air of breezy indifference.

"That is the ugliest car I have ever seen," Felicity said.

"Why do you think your opinion would mean anything to me?" I asked.

"You're going to pretend you like driving that thing?" Felicity asked, tossing her hair back over her shoulders. "I wouldn't be caught dead in it."

"I guess I'm just not as superficial as you are," I said.

"That's for sure," Felicity said. "Just look at the way you—"

I knew she was about to say *dress*, but then she looked me up and down and a frown darkened her face. I was wearing a navy and white striped tank top that tied behind my neck with my new khaki cargo miniskirt. The tank top on its own wasn't strictly dress code compliant, so I'd brought a cotton navy cardigan to wear over it for when I got out of the heat. Hannah, of course, had helped me pick out my outfit for the first day of school. Actually, it had been a little insulting, as Hannah had insisted on not only selecting my clothes, but then actually laying them out on the floor with accessories—a trio of silver bangles and a necklace with a bird-shaped pendant—so that I wouldn't make any mistakes while dressing.

I'd always thought that there wasn't any point in getting all dressed up just to go sit in a classroom all day. But I had to admit, it felt pretty good to silence Felicity Glen.

"What were you going to say?" I asked sweetly. "Something about the way I dress?"

"Whatever. I don't have time to stand around talking to you all day," Felicity said, turning away. "And your car is hideous!"

I laughed at her departing back.

"Should I be worried that you're standing here by yourself,

laughing?" Charlie asked, appearing beside me. "You're not having a nervous breakdown, are you?"

Charlie was one of my best friends. She was thin and her short, spiky hair was bright green. Today, she was wearing a purple tunic with a pink satin skirt over a black tulle underskirt. Somehow, Charlie managed to make it all look incredibly stylish.

"Green?" I asked. The last time I'd seen her—two days ago—her hair had been Strawberry Shortcake red.

"I thought I'd shake things up for the first day of school," Charlie explained. "So, are you having a nervous breakdown?"

"No," I said. "Just enjoying giving Felicity a smack down, thanks to my awesome new fashion skills."

Charlie looked me over. "You are looking especially cute this morning. Did Hannah dress you?"

"No, I dressed myself, thank you very much," I said.

"But she picked out your clothes, right?"

"Do you really have so little faith in my fashion sense?"

"Yes," Charlie said.

"Thanks a lot," I said.

"You're the one who always says you were born without a fashion gene," Charlie said, shrugging. "Have you seen Finn yet?"

Charlie's tone was casual, but I knew better. Finn was our other best friend. Over the summer, Charlie had finally admitted to me what I'd long suspected—that she had feelings for Finn that went beyond friendship. I'd had reason to believe that Finn had similar feelings for Charlie. But it was a case of bad timing—Finn currently had a girlfriend, Phoebe McLeod, who was in Hannah's class at Orange Cove High. He was also oblivious to Charlie's feelings for him. I'd advised Charlie to just tell Finn how she felt about him, but so far she'd refused to do so. She was convinced that if she told Finn she had feelings for him, things between them would become awkward and strained and eventually ruin their friendship.

"Not yet," I said as we walked up the sidewalk, which snaked from the student parking lot around the side of the school. "But I did talk to him briefly last night. He said he has a surprise for us."

"Uh-oh," Charlie said.

"Yeah, that was pretty much my reaction, too," I said.

Finn was very funny and completely brilliant, but he also lacked a moral compass. His idea of a surprise could mean an announcement that he had hacked into the Federal Reserve and transferred ten billion dollars to an offshore account. He was totally capable of doing it—Finn was a computer genius who'd developed several top-selling video games. In a review, a critic had called Finn's most famous creation, Grunge Aliens, "the most awesomely violent video game ever made." Finn had been thrilled. Anyway, his series of successful computer games meant that Finn was set for life, and didn't have to worry about getting into a top college or landing a good job postgraduation. So there was even less incentive for him to stay out of trouble.

"What do you think he's done this time?" Charlie asked, as we turned the corner and headed down the walk that led to the front entrance of Geek High.

I stopped dead in my tracks. "I think I might have an idea."

"What?" Charlie asked, also stopping. Then, following my appalled stare, she turned toward the stairs that led up to the front door. Her mouth fell open. "Please tell me I'm not seeing what I think I'm seeing."

"I would love to. But I'd be lying," I said.

Finn stood at the top of the stairs, beaming down at us. He was tall and pale, with light blue eyes and a faint scar over his lip, a remnant from the cleft-lip surgery he'd had as a baby. His brown hair used to be too long and shaggy. Now the sides were shaved, leaving one single stripe down the center of his head.

"He has a Mohawk," Charlie squeaked.

"Yes, he does. And he looks like an idiot." I looked at her. "Please tell me this has some effect on your feelings for him."

Charlie shrugged helplessly. "I wish I could say it does. But who am I to talk? I have green hair."

"But you could dye your hair back to a normal color tonight if you wanted to. He's stuck with that ridiculous look until it grows in," I protested.

Finn took the stairs two at a time and jogged out to meet us. "Hey, foxy ladies," he said. Finn preened, turning his head from side to side to give us the full view. "So? What do you think?"

"Do you really want to know?" I asked.

Finn looked hurt. "You don't like the new look?"

"No," Charlie and I said together.

"Too bad," Finn crowed. "Because I love it. My head feels so much cooler without all of the hair. And Phoebe thinks I look sexy like this."

"That's because Phoebe's a few fries short of a Happy Meal," Charlie muttered under her breath.

"What's that? I didn't hear you," Finn asked. "Were you commenting on how insanely hot I look?"

"No," Charlie said. "I was not."

"Because you can totally say that if you want to. Really, please feel free to admire the Mohawk all you want. I'll even let you touch it," Finn said, running a hand over his head.

"I'll pass," Charlie said.

"Miranda? I don't want you to feel left out," Finn said.

"No, thanks, Finn. I don't want to touch your head," I said.

"Suit yourself," Finn said.

The three of us turned toward the school, and paused for a moment before heading up the stairs. When Geek High first opened, it occupied a three-story Victorian house with large dormer windows and a gabled roof. But as the school grew, two low, modern wings were added that branched out from either side of the main building. The high school occupied one wing, and the elementary and middle schools the other, while the original central building housed the cafeteria and administrative offices.

"Another year of pointless torture is upon us," Finn said sadly.

"Just think: only two more years before we leave for college," I said, feeling a bit nostalgic.

"*Only* two?" Finn said, snorting.

"That's not so long," Charlie said. "Just imagine how strange it will be when we graduate. I can't imagine not coming here every day."

"I can," Finn said with a shudder. "I can't wait to get out of here and out into the real world. And by real world, I mean being able to sleep until noon, play Xbox all day, and eat cereal for breakfast, lunch, and dinner."

"You won't miss the people? Your friends?" Charlie asked.

"No way. I'll be sick of all of you by then," Finn said cheerfully. "Once we get our diplomas, you'll never see me again. Unless it's on the cover of *People* magazine, when I'm named Sexiest Man Alive." He winked at me. "That's one of my life goals."

"It's good to have goals," I said.

"Well, if that's the way you feel and if we really mean so little to you, why bother hanging out with us at all?" Charlie asked testily.

Finn looked at her, blinking with surprise. "Yeesh. I was just kidding. You know I love you guys."

"Whatever." Charlie looked around and spotted Padma Paswan heading into the school with Emma Cliff. "Hey, Padma! Wait up! I have to talk to you about something. See you later, Miranda."

And with a swish of pink satin and black tulle, Charlie turned and jogged up the steps to join Padma and Emma.

"What was that about?" Finn asked, still looking bewildered. "What did I say?"

I shrugged. "Not sure," I lied. "Maybe Charlie's not a fan of *People* magazine."

As Finn muttered under his breath about how he'd never understand girls, we headed up the stairs and into school together. It really was good to be back at old Geek High after the summer away. It was reassuring the way it never changed, from the stern-faced oil paintings of donors glaring down at us from the walls, to the worn oriental rugs in the front hall, to the large trophy case, which now held the Mu Alpha Theta State Championship trophy my MATh competition team won the previous spring. So much in my life had changed in the past year, what with my mom, Sadie, leaving for London, my moving in with my dad, meeting Dex, falling in love for the first time, and, finally, Dex leaving. It was nice to have something stay the same.

And then, just as this thought was flitting across my brain, I suddenly saw something different. Actually not some*thing*, but some*one*. A girl walking down the hall. She had mousy brown hair and was wearing a black T-shirt, faded cutoff jeans, black socks, and worn-looking black Doc Martens boots. The school was small, so whenever a new student came in, he or she always stood out. I had a feeling that this girl wouldn't be happy to know that. She was tall—nearly as tall as me—but walked with her head down and her shoulders slumped forward, as though she were willing herself to become invisible.

Finn was still ranting about Charlie. ". . . and I swear she said something mean about Phoebe. I didn't hear what it was exactly, but I can tell Charlie doesn't like her. Has she said anything about Phoebe to you?"

"Look," I said, poking Finn in the side to get his attention.

"What?"

"A new girl," I said.

Finn perked up. "A new girl? Where?"

"Over there. Heading into the high school wing," I said. "Do you see her? Over there in the black T-shirt."

"Oh," Finn said as he spotted her. From his tone, he was clearly underwhelmed. "Not a hottie."

I rolled my eyes. "Don't be a pig," I said.

"I can't help it," Finn said with an unconcerned shrug. "As a wise man once said, I yam what I yam."

"What wise man?" I asked suspiciously.

"Popeye," Finn said.

Chapter Three

I had Nineteenth-Century American Literature first period. Neither Finn nor Charlie had signed up for the class—Charlie had an extra art period, and Finn's exact words were, "I'd rather have my eyelashes plucked out one by one"—so I headed to Mrs. Gordon's classroom alone. Many of the same students who'd been in her Modern Literature class last year had signed up for the class. Padma and Emma were both there, along with Tate Metcalf, Sanjiv Gupta, Christopher Frost, and Tabitha Stone. Unfortunately, Felicity Glen was also in the class, along with her equally annoying best friend, Morgan Simpson.

The seats, which were arranged in a semicircle, were already mostly full. There was an empty desk next to Felicity, but there was no way I was sitting next to her. I glanced around and spotted an empty seat between Sanjiv and the new girl. I swallowed back a sigh. Sitting next to Sanjiv wasn't much of an improvement over Felicity—he was a stress case and obsessed with the Mu Alpha Theta competition team—but at least Sanjiv wouldn't spend the period hurling whispered insults at me. It was an easy choice.

"Hi, Sanjiv," I said, sitting down at the empty desk next to his.

Sanjiv had gotten even taller and ganglier over the summer, and his Adam's apple had grown more prominent. He pushed his over-sized, metal-rimmed glasses up his nose, and said, "Hi, Miranda. The first MATh team meeting is being held this Thursday."

Uh-oh, I thought. I knew I was eventually going to have to break the news to Sanjiv that I wasn't going to be on the Mu Alpha Theta team—MATh for short—this year. I just hadn't thought I'd have to do it before the first class on the first day of the school year had even begun.

"Um, actually, I'm not going to be on the MATh team this year," I said. "Sorry."

And I really was sorry. I hadn't wanted to be on the team the previous year, either—long story, but basically the Geek High headmaster blackmailed me into it—but even so, I had grown fond of my MATh teammates over the year and I was proud that we'd won at State.

Sanjiv stared at me in horrified disbelief, his Adam's apple bobbing furiously in his throat. "Not be on the team?" he croaked. "But you have to be! We can't win State again without you!"

"I just can't. I'm going to be writing for *The Ampersand*, which is a really big time commitment," I said apologetically. "I don't have any room in my schedule for MATh team."

I'd been thrilled when I found out I'd gotten one of the few coveted spots on *The Ampersand*. In fact, it was the main reason I hadn't moved to London to live with Sadie this year. My biggest dream was to someday be a writer. And not a writer like my mom, who wrote paperback novels featuring eighteenth-century heroines whose dresses were being pulled off by long-haired cads—not that there was anything wrong with writing to entertain. But I wanted to write something serious, something that would make a difference. I wanted to write the Great American Novel, in the tradition of John Steinbeck, F. Scott Fitzgerald, and J. D. Salinger. And as far as I was concerned, getting published in *The Ampersand* would be the first step toward this goal. I was hoping that if I got one of my short stories published in our prestigious school magazine, it might help me secure a spot at one of the top college writing programs.

"This can't be happening. It can't. It's a nightmare. Does Leila know? Does Kyle?" Sanjiv moaned. Kyle and Leila were also on the MATh team, but they weren't nearly as hard-core about it as Sanjiv. I was fairly sure they wouldn't take my defection quite as badly as he was taking it.

"I don't know," I said apologetically.

Sanjiv lapsed into silence, his head on his hands, moaning occasionally. Embarrassed, I looked away. The new girl was sitting quietly on my other side, her laptop out, ready for class to begin. When I glanced over, she was looking in my direction, obviously eavesdropping on my conversation with Sanjiv. When I caught her eye, she flushed a dark red and looked away quickly, her shoulders hunching up.

"Hi," I said. "I'm Miranda."

The girl glanced back at me, as though wanting to make sure I was speaking to her. I smiled encouragingly.

"Hi," she finally said. "I'm Nora."

Finn was right: Nora was not a hottie, but I didn't think she was unattractive. She was just plain, with unremarkable features—brown eyes, a slightly rounded nose, thin lips, mousy hair. Her best feature was her clear, ivory skin.

"You're new here, right?" I said.

She nodded. "I just moved here from Boston."

"Cool," I said. "Did you go to a Geek High there, too?"

Nora looked at me blankly. I realized she hadn't been here long enough to pick up the shorthand.

"Geek High is what everyone in town calls Notting Hill," I explained. "Because of the IQ requirement to get in."

"Oh," Nora said, blushing again. "No. I went to a regular school. But I was in the Gifted and Talented program there."

Before I could respond, Felicity Glen's carrying voice cut across the room: "Oh, my *God*. Is that girl actually wearing Doc Martens? Does she think it's 1993 or something?" she said, while Morgan snickered sycophantically.

I glared daggers at Felicity. She smirked back at me, causing me to indulge in a brief but satisfying fantasy of picturing what Felicity would look like if all of her hair fell out and her face was covered in angry red pimples.

"Ignore her," I advised Nora. "Felicity is one hundred percent pure evil. Seriously, I'm pretty sure she spends her free time kicking kindergartners."

But Nora had stopped blushing. Instead, all of the color had drained from her face, leaving her skin a sickly paper white. She stared down at her computer screen, blinking hard, as though she were fighting back tears. I tried to think of something comforting to say, but just then, Mrs. Gordon walked in, and a beat later, the bell rang, signaling the beginning of class.

"Hello, everyone! I hope you all had a nice summer," Mrs. Gordon said, closing the door behind her.

Mrs. Gordon was my favorite teacher at Geek High. She was plump, with wispy hair that was forever falling out of an old-fashioned bun. Today she was wearing a yellow cardigan that was misbuttoned, and a floral skirt that had what looked like a coffee stain near the hem. But she had a kind smile, and her literature classes were the academic high point of my day.

"Welcome to Nineteenth-Century American Literature. We're

going to start with an old favorite of mine," Mrs. Gordon continued. She reached into the box on her desk and pulled out a paperback book. "*The Adventures of Tom Sawyer*. Tate, will you pass out the books for me?"

While Tate grabbed a stack of books out of the box and began handing them around, I shot Nora a sideways glance. She still looked miserable. Her eyes were downcast and she was chewing on her lower lip. When she took the book Tate held out to her, I could see that her hand was shaking slightly. I felt another hot rush of anger toward Felicity. It was one thing for Felicity to pick on me—I knew what kind of person she was, so her opinion meant nothing to me. But to pick on poor Nora, who was new at Geek High and probably didn't have a single friend here, was just plain mean.

Felicity apparently felt the weight of my gaze, because she turned to stare at me, raising her eyebrows provocatively. I rolled me eyes in disgust and looked away.

"*Tom Sawyer* is set in the antebellum South in the fictional town of St. Petersburg," Mrs. Gordon said. "It's a classic coming-of-age story. Has anyone read it?"

A few hands went up, including Tabitha Stone's. Tabitha was widely seen as the literary genius of Geek High, largely because she'd had a book of poetry published two years earlier. I'd read her poems and wasn't that impressed. Besides, Tabitha took herself way too seriously.

Tabitha kept her hand up, and Mrs. Gordon nodded at her.

"I think one of the most compelling themes in *Tom Sawyer* is the hypocrisy of the establishment. The church, the law, Tom's school," Tabitha said, sounding as condescending as ever.

"That's true. But let's not get ahead of ourselves," Mrs. Gordon said. "Today I'll introduce the book to you—the setting, the main characters, the historical background—so you'll have a point of reference when you begin reading."

Tabitha looked disgruntled. She loved showing off, and obviously resented not being praised for her superior knowledge.

Feeling cheered up, I opened my laptop and began taking notes.

♦

When the bell rang, signaling the end of class, there was the usual flurry of activity. Laptops were stowed away, book bags were zipped up, people began chatting. By the time I'd packed up my things and turned around, Nora was gone. She must have scurried out of the classroom first thing.

I kept an eye out for Nora for the rest of the morning, but we didn't have any other classes together. I had independent study for math with Mr. Gordon—husband of Mrs. Gordon and the coach for the math team—then, after math, I had physics with Mr. Forrester. Finn and Charlie were both taking physics with me, and Charlie was still visibly annoyed at Finn. I shared a table with Charlie, and we sat behind Finn and his buddy, Tate Metcalf.

I didn't see Nora until lunchtime. Lunch at Geek High was served family style. The cafeteria staff set out platters of sandwiches, crudités, and cookies on each round table and everyone helped themselves. This was meant to foster a sense of camaraderie between the students, but instead, there's such competition to get to the edible sandwiches (turkey, ham, chicken club) and avoid the inedible ones (tuna, egg salad, pimento loaf) that Geek High students have been known to rush the lunch room and dive at the platters. You'd think the cafeteria staff would have noticed the strong preferences, but if they did, it didn't move them to make any changes to the menu. Maybe they enjoyed sadistically torturing us with goopy brown tuna salad studded with chunks of soggy celery.

During the usual mad dash into the lunch room, I saw Nora standing to one side, looking lost and a little overwhelmed at the swarm of activity around the lunch tables. I fought my way through the crowd and headed over to her.

"Hi," I said. "Do you want to sit with us?"

Nora hesitated, still chewing on her bottom lip, but finally she nodded.

"It gets crazy in here at lunchtime," I said as I led her to the table where Finn and Charlie were already seated, carefully guarding a platter of chicken club sandwiches.

"Yeah, I noticed," Nora said.

"It's the natural consequence of limited supply and increased demand. Just avoid the egg salad at all costs. Trust me." I slid into an empty seat next to Finn, and gestured for Nora to sit next to me. "Nora, this is Finn and Charlie. Guys, this is Nora."

Finn gave Nora a smart salute and said, "S'up?"

Charlie smiled at her and said, "Hi, Nora."

"Hi," Nora said shyly.

"You're new here, right? How's your first day going?" Charlie asked.

"It's fine," Nora said unconvincingly. "I'm just trying to learn my way around."

"Has the official hazing started yet?" Finn asked.

"Hazing?" Nora repeated nervously.

"No one's told you about that? Whoops, my bad. Forget I said anything. You'll find out soon enough," Finn said menacingly, although he softened the effect with a goofy wriggle of his eyebrows.

"Just ignore him. There's no hazing," I told Nora, handing her the platter of sandwiches. Finn made a wild grab for the last chicken club. I quickly moved it out of his way. "Finn! You've already had three!"

"I'm a growing boy. I need nourishment," Finn complained.

"Then have a tuna," I said.

"Thanks, but I'd rather eat glass," Finn said.

"There's an idea," Charlie said. "Go for it."

Nora pushed the plate back toward Finn. "It's okay. You can have it. I'm not that hungry."

"Wa-hoo," Finn said. He grabbed for the last sandwich and stuffed it whole in his mouth. It was so large, he could barely fit it all in. Charlie and I stared at him with twin expressions of disgust.

"That is so gross," Charlie said.

It took Finn a few minutes to chew and swallow. When he could finally talk, he asked Charlie, "Why all the abuse today? Did I unknowingly run over your dog or something?"

Charlie looked momentarily flustered, and then—even more surprisingly—she actually *blushed*. I couldn't remember ever seeing Charlie blush before.

"I don't have a dog, you idiot," she muttered.

"Seriously, what gives?" Finn pressed on. "You've been crabby all day. Oh, wait—are you having one of your special girl days?"

"Finn!" I said. I inclined my head toward Nora. "Can you please behave? We have company."

"So what?" he asked. "There's no reason to be ashamed of your bodily functions, Miranda."

"So, Nora," Charlie said, raising her voice to cut Finn off. "Where are you from?"

"Boston," Nora said.

"And your family moved here?"

"Actually, no. Just me," Nora said. We all looked at her curiously. I got the feeling she didn't want to go into the details of her relocation. Finally, reluctantly, Nora continued. "My grandmother lives here. I'm staying with her."

"Why?" Finn asked. "Wait, no, let me guess. Your parents are witnesses in a high-profile federal prosecution of the godfather of a crime syndicate. They're entering the Witness Protection Program, but you decided you didn't want to live out the rest of your life under an assumed identity. Am I right?"

We all stared at Finn.

"What?" he asked. "It's possible."

"Um, no. That's not why I moved here," Nora said.

"So, give us the details. Did you get kicked out of your old school? Oh, snap—did you call in a bomb threat? I actually considered that once, but the potential consequences if you get caught—you know, a criminal record, jail time—outweighed the benefit of getting out of school for the day," Finn continued.

Nora, who didn't know that Finn was never serious about anything, started to look a little frightened. I kicked Finn under the table to shut him up.

"Ow! You kicked me!" he said indignantly.

"Maybe Nora doesn't want to talk about why she moved here," I said.

"There's no need for violence," Finn said. "I was just making polite conversation."

"You wouldn't know polite conversation if it bit you on the—" Charlie began.

I cut her off before she could finish the thought. "How do you like Geek High so far, Nora?"

"It's okay," Nora said without any enthusiasm whatsoever. "The work seems a lot more advanced than at my old school. I hope I can keep up."

"Really?" Finn asked interestedly. "Maybe I should transfer out of here. I wouldn't mind an easier workload."

"Like you ever do any of the work, anyway," Charlie scoffed.

"That's true. I rarely see the point of homework. But if I did ever choose to do it, it would be nice to have a soft option," Finn said.

"You'll have to do your physics homework," I said. "You heard what Mr. Forrester said. Homework counts as twenty percent of the final grade. If you don't hand it in, you won't pass the class."

Finn waved his hand dismissively. "Pass, schmass. Who cares?"

"So I guess this isn't the year when you're going to start taking academics seriously?" Charlie asked.

Finn shook his head regretfully. "Sadly, no." He reached for a peanut butter cookie, and then grimaced once he'd taken a bite. "Stale," he said.

"The food here really is shockingly bad," Charlie said. "Miranda, you should write an exposé on it for *The Ampersand*."

"That's the school magazine," I explained to Nora. "I'm going to write for it this year."

"So what do you think of my idea? The horrors of the Geek High cafeteria exposed," Charlie said.

"First of all, I don't think we get to pick our assignments. The editor in chief does that. And, anyway, I'm not really interested in writing an exposé," I said.

"Why? What do you want to write?" Charlie asked.

"Fiction," I said. "There's always at least one fiction piece per edition."

"Hmm," Charlie said. She looked like she wanted to say something, but decided against it. Instead, she picked up a carrot stick and chewed thoughtfully on it.

"What?" I asked.

"Nothing," Charlie said.

"Come on, just spit it out."

"It's just that I've heard there's a lot of competition for the fiction spot," she said.

"Where'd you hear that from?" I asked.

"Tabitha Stone," Charlie admitted.

"Uh-oh," Finn said, continuing to eat the stale peanut butter cookie.

"What?" I asked.

"You've always had a problem with Tabitha Stone," Finn said.

"No, I haven't," I said.

"Yes, you have," Charlie and Finn said together.

I glowered at both of them. It figured that the first time the two of them had gotten along all day was at my expense.

"Just because I don't particularly *like* Tabitha doesn't mean I have a problem with her," I said loftily.

Charlie and Finn exchanged a meaningful glance. Nora watched all of us from underneath lowered lashes.

"Face it, M. You've been jealous of Tabitha ever since she had that book of poetry published," Finn said.

"*Self*-published," I corrected him. "Her dad paid for it to be published. Anyone can do that. There's nothing to be jealous of."

"Whatever," Finn said, shrugging.

"No, not *whatever*," I said. I could feel my temper gaining heat. "That's what happened."

"I thought her book received positive reviews," Charlie said. "In fact, wasn't it mentioned in the *New York Times Book Review*?"

"So? It was still self-published!" I said.

"Relax, Miranda. All I'm saying is that having a publishing credit has got to work in Tabitha's favor. I don't want you to be disappointed if she's picked to write the fiction piece for the fall issue," Charlie said.

"So you think Tabitha is going to be picked over me?" I asked indignantly. "Thanks for the support!"

After all, I'd been a finalist in the Winston Creative Writing

Contest. Sure, I hadn't won, but that was because I hadn't been able to attend the finals. They were held the same weekend as the Mu Alpha Theta state finals, and the Geek High MATh team would have been disqualified for being a player short if I hadn't gone with them. But surely being a finalist in a prestigious national writing contest was just as impressive as paying someone to publish your maudlin, incomprehensible poetry.

"You know I'm your biggest fan," Charlie said. "Finn, too."

"Actually, not so much—" Finn began. But before he could finish, he said, "Ouch! Why do you guys keep kicking me?"

"Sorry," Charlie said sweetly. She turned to Nora, who had been watching us all silently but intently. "So, Nora. What's on your schedule?"

"This is her not-so-subtle attempt to change the subject," I told Nora.

Nora stood abruptly. "Actually, I have to go," she said.

We all looked up at her in surprise. There were still fifteen minutes left before the bell rang.

"I have to see my guidance counselor. I was put in a biology class, but I already took that at my old school," Nora explained.

"So? If you take it again, you'll ace it without having to do any of the work," Finn said.

"But she'd have to do the frog dissection again," Charlie reminded him.

"So? Big deal," Finn said.

Charlie and I both snorted with laughter.

"Finn, you threw up during the frog dissection unit," I reminded him.

"I did not!"

"Yes, you did, too," Charlie said, giggling. "It was classic."

"Lies. It's all lies, I tell you," Finn said.

Nora shifted from foot to foot, looking like she wanted to flee.

"Good luck with the guidance counselor," I said.

"Thanks. Bye," Nora said. She tucked her head, turned, and hurried off, her shoulders hunched and one hand gripping the strap of her backpack.

"She's a bit of an odd duck," Finn said.

"I think she's nice," I said. "She's just shy. Right, Charlie?"

Charlie shrugged. "Hard to tell. She barely spoke."

"She's odd," Finn said again. "And those are the ones you have to worry about. They seem quiet and nice, and then the police end up finding fifteen corpses buried under the floorboards of their house. And everyone says, 'She seemed so nice. Just a little shy.'"

"You," I said to him, "are deeply, deeply troubled."

I stood, shouldering my backpack.

"Now where are you going?" Finn asked. "Why is everyone running off? Lunch is only half over."

"I have some things to do," I said. After they'd ganged up on me, accusing me of being jealous of Tabitha, I didn't want to tell them I was going to the library to get a head start on my proposal for *The Ampersand*. The first meeting was tomorrow afternoon, and I was going to make sure I was super prepared. Tabitha Stone wouldn't know what hit her.

Chapter Four

That night, after dinner, Dex called me on Skype. We'd made plans to talk at seven o'clock sharp, so I was in my room, sitting cross-legged on my bed with my laptop balanced on my knees when his call beeped in. Willow, my brindle greyhound, was stretched out on a white flokati rug on the floor beside me, fast asleep. Her feet were twitching, and she was grunting happily. I wondered whether she was dreaming of being back at the racetrack, chasing a mechanical rabbit.

"Hi!" I said, when Dex's face appeared on my computer screen.

Dex had pale skin, a smattering of freckles, and smiling blue eyes. His coppery red hair had grown out over the summer, and was now just the slightest bit shaggy. I could tell Dex was calling from his dorm room, which had block concrete walls painted a sickly lime green. He'd taped up a poster of a surfer riding a huge wave.

"Hi!" Dex said.

Neither one of us spoke for a long moment, and then we both started talking at once.

"How was practice?" I asked.

"How was your first day of school?" Dex asked.

We both stopped and laughed. Willow lifted her head at the sound of Dex's voice, and her tail thumped a few times.

"You first," Dex said, smiling his crooked smile.

"How was practice today?" I asked.

In Orange Cove, school started in August. But at Dex's new boarding school in Maine, classes didn't begin until September. Dex had gone to school early with the rest of his new lacrosse team for summer training camp.

"Coach put us through our paces today," Dex said. "We ran wind sprints until Matt Heneberry puked."

"Ugh. Is that even legal? It sounds like torture," I said.

"It's supposed to build character," Dex said.

"I have all the character I need, thanks," I said. I'm allergic to exercise in general, and running in particular.

"At least it's a lot cooler up here. It would have been ten times worse in the heat. We'd all have been throwing up," Dex said.

"Remember that this winter when you're snowed in," I said.

Dex laughed. "That's true. There won't be any surfing in the middle of January for me, that's for sure."

"Have you been able to surf there?" I asked.

Dex was an amazingly good surfer. He even parasailed, which was surfing while strapped to a parachute.

Dex shook his head. "No, I didn't even bring my board. We're nowhere near the ocean."

"That's too bad," I said sympathetically.

"Tell me about it. I really miss it," Dex said. He hesitated, and although he was still smiling, I thought his eyes looked sad. "And I really miss you."

Warm zings shot through me. Dex had always had this effect on me.

"I miss you, too," I said softly.

Dex looked over his shoulder, as though checking to make sure that he was really alone. His roommate, Jake, was also a lacrosse player. Dex seemed to like him well enough, but I didn't get the sense that they were close. Dex leaned closer to his computer and, keeping his voice low, he said, "Can I tell you something?"

"Of course. You can tell me anything. Well, almost anything. Just as long as it doesn't have anything to do with vomit. Just hearing someone else talk about throwing up always makes me want to hurl," I said. "I also don't deal well with body piercings, especially in the nose."

"No, this isn't vomit or piercing related," Dex said.

"Then shoot."

"I think coming here might have been a mistake," he said.

I couldn't help the surge of hopefulness that bubbled up inside me. Maybe Dex would decide to leave boarding school and come back home to Orange Cove! But almost as soon as this thought popped into my mind, I tried to will it away. "I think it's totally normal to go through an adjustment period. Give it time. I'm sure it will get better," I said.

"I guess," Dex said, looking unconvinced.

"I thought you said you liked the guys on your team."

"I do. They're pretty cool for the most part." Dex shrugged the subject away. "Anyway, let's talk about something else. Tell me about your day. How was being back at school? Is the brainpower still running at warp speed?"

I'd always been a little uncomfortable talking about the genius factor at Geek High with anyone who didn't go there. Even Dex. It seemed braggy, as though I were waving my arms in the air and announcing, "Look at me! I'm a genius!" The truth was that next to some of my classmates, I felt completely ordinary.

"Pretty much the same as always," I said. Then, remembering Nora, I added, "Although there is a new girl in my class. I felt so bad for her. She seemed really shy and nervous, and Felicity Glen was being horrible to her."

"Yeah, it sucks to be the new kid in school," Dex said.

"No one's being horrible to you, are they?" I asked. It was easy to see why Nora would have a tough time—she was so shy and awkward. Dex was just the opposite. He was so outgoing and funny and laid-back, it was impossible to imagine anyone not liking him.

"Nah. It's just harder when you don't really know anyone. I've known most of my Orange Cove friends since kindergarten. We know each other's families; know the same inside jokes. When you're the new kid, it's just completely different. You're always playing catch-up," Dex explained.

I hated the thought of Dex feeling like an outsider, and wondered if Nora felt the same way.

Probably, I thought. I should make more of an effort to befriend her. Even if she was, as Finn said, a bit odd.

"How's Bumblebee?" Dex asked. Bumblebee was his nickname for my car. "Have you gotten rid of the smell yet?"

It was true. My car *did* smell. It was an unpleasant odor, a mixture of fast-food grease and body odor. It had been there when my dad first gave it to me a few weeks earlier, and I'd hoped that, over time, it would dissipate. But if anything, rather than going away, the stink just got stronger.

"No. I sprayed down the interior with two bottles of Lysol, but it didn't make a dent," I said.

"Lysol? That's not going to cut it with a stink like that. You need some sort of industrial-strength smell cleanser," Dex said. He laughed, and I was glad to see that his smile was now reaching his eyes.

"Where would I find something like that?" I asked.

"I don't know. Is there a toxic-waste cleaning service in Orange Cove? Maybe they could help," Dex suggested.

*

After I got off Skype, I was feeling out of sorts. I missed Dex. And hearing that he was considering leaving school and returning home just made it that much worse. As much as I missed him and wanted him to come back, his scholarship to the Brown Academy really was too good of an opportunity for him to pass up.

I shut my laptop and headed off to find Hannah. She was in her lilac-painted room, sitting behind a white lacquered desk, typing away on her laptop.

"Hey. Are you busy?" I asked, hesitating at the door.

Hannah looked up. "Not really. Do you know anything about computers?"

"Just the basics. Why, is your laptop broken?" I asked, taking a seat on the edge of her white canopy bed.

"No, it's fine. I need to start a Web site," Hannah said.

"For what?"

Hannah frowned at me. "What do you think?"

I tried to think of what she was up to lately that would require a Web site, and came up blank.

"Seriously, I have no idea," I said. "Give me a hint."

"My new matchmaking business," Hannah said.

"Oh, right," I said. I'd forgotten about Hannah's new project. She'd decided to start a matchmaking service for Orange Cove High School students. It all started over the summer when she tried to help Charlie attract Finn's attention. The fact that it didn't work out, and that Finn continued to date his bubbleheaded girlfriend, Phoebe McLeod, hadn't in any way diminished Hannah's enthusiasm for this new project. She was convinced her destiny was to be a modern-day Cupid. Minus the diaper and bag of arrows.

"Are you really at the Web site stage?" I asked.

"This is a business. Marketing is *everything*," Hannah said.

"You're going to charge people for setting them up?" I asked.

"Of course! If I don't, no one will take it seriously," Hannah said.

"So, what're you going to do? Put your clients' photos up on your Web site with a *click here if you're interested* button?" I asked.

"Please tell me you're not serious," Hannah said with a disdainful sniff.

I shrugged one shoulder. "I have no idea how dating Web sites work. Enlighten me."

"First of all, it's not a dating Web site. Those are for losers," Hannah said.

"Very nice," I said sarcastically.

"We're offering a professional matchmaking service that will give our clients individualized attention as we help them find the perfect, high-quality boyfriend or girlfriend," Hannah said, looking pleased with herself. I had the feeling she'd practiced this spiel. Probably in front of a mirror.

"High-quality?" I repeated. "You do know you're talking about people and not handbags, right?"

"That's your problem, Miranda. You want to believe that we live in a world where looks and popularity don't matter," Hannah said.

"I just think that there are qualities that should matter more. Like how nice a person is, or whether they have a good sense of humor," I said.

"Don't worry, we're definitely going to factor in personality," Hannah assured me. "After all, lots of pretty girls fall for average-looking guys with great personalities. Think of all the ugly rock stars out there who end up with hot wives." Her forehead furrowed. "It doesn't really work the other way, though. Good-looking guys will always pick dull, pretty girls over funny, ugly ones. I should probably make a note of that." Hannah picked up her pencil and jotted down a note in a pink patent leather notebook, muttering as she did so, "Hot guys with hot girls only. Hot girls may date down, but only if he's got a great personality." She underlined the word *great* three times.

I rolled my eyes. "That is so shallow."

"Shallow, but true," Hannah said, shutting the journal. "How's Dex? I thought I heard you talking to him."

"Yeah, I was. He's good," I said. "I guess."

"What does that mean?"

"I don't think he's very happy at school," I said.

"Really? Maybe if he hates it enough, he'll come home," Hannah suggested. "That would be cool."

"But I want him to do well. And I want him to be happy," I said.

Hannah waved an airy hand. "In that case, don't worry. I'm sure he'll be fine. He'll make friends and settle in, and then he'll probably never want to come home."

"Is that supposed to make me feel better?"

Hannah gave me an unusually sympathetic look. "That's what normally happens, Miranda," she said kindly. "Most high school couples break up when one or both of them goes off to college. They make new friends and only see their old high school friends on vacations. Dex going off to boarding school is basically the same thing."

"So you think he's going to dump me," I said as cold dread spread through my stomach.

Hannah shrugged. "You never know. Maybe he'll transfer back home before that happens."

"But he wanted to play lacrosse at Brown Academy. I think it would make him really unhappy if he doesn't succeed there," I said.

"But you guys would keep dating," Hannah pointed out.

"So those are my two options? Getting dumped or staying together, but with Dex feeling like a failure?"

"Basically," Hannah said.

I slumped back on her bed, feeling utterly dejected. Hannah def-

initely knew what she was talking about when it came to relationships.

"Look on the bright side," Hannah said.

"There's a bright side?"

"Absolutely. If you and Dex do break up, I'll take you on as a client and find a really nice guy to set you up with," Hannah said
brightly.

"Lucky me," I said grumpily.

"I know, right?" Hannah agreed.

Chapter Five

The next day, I looked for Nora before lit class, but she arrived just as the bell was ringing, and sat across the room from me. Then, after class was over, she disappeared while I was packing up my laptop. I did notice that Nora had traded her Doc Martens for a pair of flip-flops, the preferred footwear for most Geek High students.

She's making an effort to fit in, I thought.

After lit class, I didn't see Nora for the rest of the day, not even at lunch. This was unusual for Geek High. It was such a small school, you were constantly running into everyone in the hallways or at lunch.

But thoughts of Nora were quickly swept away by my increasing nervousness over my first meeting with the staff of *The Ampersand*. It was scheduled for that afternoon after school. I really wanted to impress the editor in chief, Candace Ruckman. Candace was a senior, and I'd always found her incredibly intimidating. She had blue-black hair that she wore long with straight bangs, had piercing blue eyes, and was coolly self-possessed.

It felt like butterflies were dive-bombing one another in my stomach as I made my way to *The Ampersand* office after the final bell rang. I must have been walking extra slowly, because by the time I got there, there were already a dozen staffers milling around. Some were just sitting and chatting together at the two rows of tables set up in the middle of the office, while others were buzzing around busily, making copies or paging through back copies of *The Ampersand*.

I took a seat and looked for Candace. She was sitting at a long table set up in the front of the room, looking unflappable. One of the staff writers, Jimmy Torres, was talking to her animatedly, gesticulating with his hands as he made a point. Candace nodded serenely and murmured something in reply, and Jimmy turned and bounded away, a big smile on his face.

Candace stood and gazed out at us with a pleasant smile. She was wearing a crisply ironed, blue button-down oxford tucked into cuffed khaki shorts. Her lips were the perfect shade of raspberry pink. I wondered whether this was natural, or if she was wearing lipstick. *If Hannah were here, she'd know*, I thought.

"Can everyone please take a seat? Then we'll get started," Candace said. Even though she barely raised her voice—which was low and husky—she instantly commanded everyone's attention. Candace waited for a moment while people took their seats at the long tables, and then smiled again. "Welcome to our first *Ampersand* staff meeting. I'm really excited about the upcoming year. Our theme this year will be"—Candace paused, allowing suspense to build— "the modern student." She smiled, allowing this announcement to sink in.

Candace continued. "We want to present our readers with a look at what it's like to be a high school student today. The challenges we face; the issues that excite us. In our first issue, we're going to focus on problems facing students. And I hope you're all excited to get to work, because I'm about to hand out your first assignments." Candace picked up a lined legal pad off the table.

I looked up quickly. She'd already made story assignments? I hadn't yet had a chance to tell Candace I'd like to be considered for the short story. Was I already too late?

"Many of you have already talked to me about what you'd like to write about, so I tried to take those preferences into account when I made the assignments," Candace continued.

Gah! I thought, suddenly seized with panic. People were already lobbying for the plum assignments? How did I not know that was happening?

"The cover story this month is going to be an in-depth look at SAT preparatory programs. Are they worth the money? Is one program vastly preferable to another? Are the program administrators making irresponsible promises to students who take their courses about what they can expect in test performance? Because of the size and scope of this article, I'm going to assign two writers to it: Peter Rossi and Coleen Duchene," Candace said.

There was a smattering of applause. I glanced at Peter and Coleen, who were sitting at a table together, looking flushed and pleased. *They're both seniors, so it makes sense that they get the highest-profile assignment*, I thought. The new staff members—which included, besides me, Tabitha Stone, Padma Paswan, Nate Fox, Vida Diaz, and Marc Holland—would probably be given less-important pieces to cut our teeth on.

Candace cleared her throat. "Our second feature is going to look at the extraordinary steps some parents are taking to get their kids into college, such as hiring consultants to help them with their applications."

There was a murmuring of interest in the room. It sounded like a juicy piece. "I've decided to assign two of our new staff writers—Marc Holland and Padma Paswan—to write it. I have confidence they'll do a great job," Candace continued.

Padma let out a gasp of excitement, and Marc grinned as Nate

Fox thumped him on the back. I smiled my congratulations at Padma. I was incredibly envious that she and Marc had gotten such a great assignment, but I was glad to know that Candace wasn't reserving all of the best assignments for seniors. Maybe I'd get a good piece, too.

But as Candace continued down her list, giving a short description of each article and then assigning a writer to it, she didn't mention my name once. I still had a small bubble of hope that maybe, just maybe, I'd be assigned the fiction piece. I hadn't asked for it specifically, but the year before I had been a finalist for the prestigious Winston Creative Writing Contest. Candace knew this; in fact, it was why I'd been invited to join the staff of *The Ampersand*.

"And, finally, I'm pleased to announce that this issue's short fiction piece will be assigned to"—Candace paused for suspense.

Say my name; say my name, I begged silently. I could feel my heartbeat rising steadily, and I crossed my fingers in my lap.

"Tabitha Stone," Candace said.

My heart stopped its rapid thumping, and instead felt like it was now plummeting into my stomach. As if it wasn't bad enough that I hadn't gotten the fiction piece, it had gone to *Tabitha*, of all people. Why her? Why not me? Jealousy snaked through me, even as I applauded politely along with the rest of the staff.

Tabitha inclined her head gracefully, as though she had just been named Queen of the World and we were her groveling subjects. "Thank you for the opportunity. I shall endeavor to do my best," she said, sounding as pompous and condescending as ever. It took all my self-control not to roll my eyes.

"I think that's everyone," Candace said, putting down her notepad. "Let me know if you'd like to bounce any ideas off me. You can also talk to Mrs. Gordon. She's agreed to be our faculty adviser again this year. Her phone number is written on the whiteboard. She said to feel free to call her at home if you need any help or advice."

Wait, I thought. *Wait! What about me?* I hadn't been assigned a piece.

I looked around, trying to see whether anyone else had been left out—or noticed that my name hadn't been called—but the rest of the staff was now chatting excitedly, all eager to get to work on their articles. Apparently, I had been the only one left out. Self-doubt suddenly cratered inside of me. What if there had been some sort of a mistake when I got the letter welcoming me to *The Ampersand* staff?

Feeling like my legs had turned into wood, I made my way up to the front of the room, where Candace stood talking to Peter Rossi. I waited while Peter went on and on about his plan to enroll in an SAT prep course—even though he'd taken the test the year before—in order to get the inside scoop on what promises were being made to students.

Candace nodded a few times as he spoke, and when it became clear that he wasn't planning on winding down anytime soon, she finally broke in. "The problem is that I need the article in two weeks, so there probably isn't time for you to take the course. Instead, why don't you start by interviewing students who signed up for it last year?"

Peter looked let down—clearly he'd been relishing the idea of going undercover—but he finally agreed that considering the time limitation, this was probably the best course of action, and then he rejoined Coleen at their table. Candace turned to look at me.

"Hi," I said. "I, um, didn't get an assignment."

"You didn't?" Candace picked up her notepad and frowned down at it. "You're Miranda Bloom, right?"

"That's right," I said, feeling a combination of nerves over what was going to happen with my assignment and relief that at least Candace hadn't immediately told me that there must have been a mistake, because I wasn't on *The Ampersand* staff.

"Oh, right, here you are," Candace said, tapping the list with one finger. "I assigned you the piece on student athletes."

"Student athletes?" I repeated.

"Sure. You can pick the direction you want to go in. It can be an interview, or, if you want to stay on theme, a look at the problems facing student athletes. Whichever you want."

My first reaction was confusion. What sort of problems did student athletes face? Limited hot water in the showers? Too many pretty cheerleaders distracting them? And Geek High didn't even have student athletes. Not really. The only sports teams we had were golf and tennis, and neither was very good.

"The main thing is, I need you to keep it short. I need only five hundred words, maximum. It's basically going to be a filler item," Candace continued.

"Right," I said, absorbing this newest blow. Tabitha Stone got the fiction feature. Marc and Padma were assigned the second-most-important feature article. I got five hundred words to be used as filler. It would probably be stuck somewhere in the back of the magazine, on the same page as an advertisement for car insurance.

"Are you all set? You know what you're doing?" Candace asked.

I nodded, wondering whether I looked as disappointed as I felt.

"Great," Candace said, and she turned to talk to Padma, who had lined up behind me, eagerly waiting to discuss her new story assignment with the editor in chief.

◆

"You're upset," Charlie said.

I nodded and stared gloomily down at my coffee mug. I'd called Charlie after the disastrous *Ampersand* meeting, and we'd arranged to meet at our favorite coffee shop, Grounded.

"I got the worst assignment," I said. "And meanwhile, everyone else—Tabitha, Padma, Marc, everyone—got great ones."

"Come on, not everyone," Charlie said. "There are always lots of short pieces in *The Ampersand*. You can't be the only one who was assigned one."

Typical Charlie, I thought. She had a habit of being annoyingly reasonable.

I shrugged. "Well, maybe not everyone got a great assignment. But I definitely got the worst one," I said grudgingly.

Charlie ran a hand through her green hair, which caused it to stick up on end like a troll doll. Somehow, she still managed to look adorable.

"What you have to do is spin this in your favor," she said.

"What does that mean?"

"Knock your article out of the park. Make it a slam dunk. Drive it off the tee." Charlie giggled, amused by her own sports-related metaphors. I shot her my best death-ray glare. "Seriously, Miranda. Look at this as an opportunity to impress your editor. If you ace this assignment—" She dissolved into giggles again.

I stood up. "If you're going to keep making sports jokes, I'm leaving."

"Okay, I promise I'll stop now," Charlie said.

I sat back down.

"What I'm trying to say is, if you do really well on this article, I'm sure Candace will give you a better assignment next time."

"How, exactly, am I supposed to impress her with a filler piece on a problem facing nonexistent student athletes? I can hardly do an exposé on steroid use in five hundred words," I complained.

"You'll think of something," Charlie said.

"How? I've got nothing. Seriously, I'm drawing a complete blank."

"Well, when I'm in the middle of a painting and get stuck, sometimes it helps if I put it aside and don't think about it for a while," Charlie suggested.

"So I'm supposed to think up a great idea by not thinking about it?" I asked doubtfully.

"The idea is that your subconscious mind continues to engage, while you distract your conscious mind. And then when you're feeling happy and relaxed, good ideas will start flowing in," Charlie said.

"I don't know," I said.

"Try it. It works for me," Charlie said.

The bell that hung on the glass-front door jingled. Charlie, who was facing toward the door, looked up. Her expression darkened. I twisted around in my seat to see who had come in. It was Finn, who had one long arm slung awkwardly around Phoebe's shoulders.

"Great," Charlie said. "Just what I need."

Finn's girlfriend was tall with long legs, which she was showing off in a very short cheerleader's outfit, and shoulder-length red hair that was pulled back in a high, bouncy ponytail secured with a blue ribbon. She was looking up at Finn and giggling at whatever he was saying.

"Does that girl ever stop laughing?" Charlie asked, her tone caustic.

"She does seem very happy," I said.

Charlie snorted. "I've met Barbie dolls who are more on the ball than that chick. She's so vapid, she makes me sick. And Finn, too, for dating her. For God's sake, she's a cheerleader."

"It's not healthy how you're always holding in your feelings. You should let them out from time to time," I said.

My sarcasm was rewarded with an extremely dirty look.

"Look, Charlie. I think you need to accept that this is happening. Even if you don't see what the attraction is, Finn really likes her," I said, leaning forward and keeping my voice low. Finn and Phoebe were still up at the counter, placing their order, but I didn't want to take the chance I'd be overheard. "He seems really happy. I don't think they're going to break up anytime soon."

"Ouch," Charlie said, her shoulders slumping.

I nodded sympathetically. "I know. Trust me, I know." And I did know. I'd been devastated when Hannah and Emmett first started dating. "But I think once you accept that she's not going anywhere anytime soon, the better off you'll be."

Charlie was quiet for a long time. I glanced over at Finn, who had finally realized we were there. He raised a hand.

"Greetings and salutations," he said.

"Hey, Finn," I said. "Hi, Phoebe."

"Hi," Phoebe said, waving.

"We'd join you, but Phoebe and I want to spend some quality time together before cheerleading practice starts," Finn said, pointing at his girlfriend with two fingers.

"I didn't know you'd joined the cheerleading squad, Finn," Charlie said.

"Very funny," Finn said.

"There are guys on our squad," Phoebe said. "They hold us up during the lifts."

"But do they get to have pom-poms?" Finn asked.

"No. Only the girls have pom-poms," Phoebe said, seemingly unaware that Finn was joking around.

Charlie smirked, and nudged me under the table.

"Two lattes, one skinny, one full fat, and one slice of carrot cake," the barista at the counter called out.

"That's us. Catch you ladies later," Finn said, turning to grab the proffered plastic tray.

"Bye!" Phoebe said perkily.

They turned and went to sit at a table by the window.

"Don't stare at them," I instructed Charlie.

"I can't help it," Charlie said. "She's feeding him carrot cake off her fork."

"So?"

"So it's hideous. And I think proximity to Phoebe is causing Finn's IQ to drop. Maybe she's a succubus," Charlie remarked.

"A succubus drains away her victim's life energy, not intelligence," I said.

"Okay, then, she's an intelligence succubus. I have to get out of here," Charlie said, standing. "Are you ready to go?"

"Sure," I said. I actually wanted to talk more about my disappointing *Ampersand* assignment, but as long as Phoebe continued feeding Finn carrot cake in full view, I wasn't going to get the best out of Charlie.

Chapter Six

I was still determined to befriend Nora, but she continued to elude me. She walked into Mrs. Gordon's Nineteenth-Century American Literature class just as the bell was ringing and disappeared as soon as class was over. As lit was the only class we had together, I didn't expect to see Nora again for the rest of the day, unless I happened to bump into her at lunch. So I was surprised when, just as we were waiting for physics class to begin, she walked in.

She headed straight for Mr. Forrester's desk and handed the teacher a note. He took it from her, looked it over, and then gave her a curt nod.

"Take a seat," Mr. Forrester said.

Charlie, who was sitting next to me, nudged me.

"I think that new girl is joining the class," she whispered.

"I didn't think we were allowed to switch classes once the semester started," I replied.

Charlie shrugged. "Maybe the rules are different if you're new."

Nora turned and nervously looked around for an open seat. Because we so frequently worked with partners in physics, we sat at tables instead of desks. Each table had room for two students. Charlie and I shared a table at the back of the room. Finn sat in front of us with Tate Metcalf. The table next to ours was empty, so I waved at Nora and gestured for her to come sit next to us. She gave me a grateful smile and slid into the empty seat.

"You can work with Charlie and me," I whispered across to her.

"Thanks," Nora whispered back.

I smiled at her, but before I could say anything else, the bell rang. Mr. Forrester stood, clearing his throat wetly. Forrester was a thin, stooped man who favored short-sleeve, button-down shirts—today's was a hideous brownish yellow—tucked into adjustable-waist pants.

"Today we're going to begin the fascinating study of kinematics," Mr. Forrester said. He held his hands in front of him, fingers spread, looking like a magician about to perform a trick.

"Sounds absolutely thrilling," Charlie muttered as she opened up her laptop and prepared to take notes.

◆

As I drove home from school that afternoon, I tried to pinpoint where, exactly, the smell in my yellow car was coming from.

Is it in the seats? I wondered, rolling down the window. If so, maybe having the upholstery shampooed and vacuumed would take care of the problem. The thought of having to live with the repulsive stink indefinitely was too horrible to contemplate.

I pulled out of the school parking lot and turned left onto the main road. Up ahead, a familiar figure was walking down the sidewalk, head down and shoulders slumped. It was Nora. I put on my signal and pulled over. Nora looked up, clearly startled.

"Hi. Do you want a ride?" I offered.

For a moment, Nora looked unsure. But then she smiled shyly and said, "Okay, thanks."

She walked around and climbed in the passenger's side. Once

she was buckled in, I pulled back out. I glanced over at her. She had an odd expression on her face while she attempted to covertly pinch her nose shut.

"I know. It's awful, right? I probably should have warned you about the stink before you got in," I said.

"It's not that bad," Nora lied unconvincingly.

"No, it really is that bad," I said, laughing. "The car came this way. I think I'm actually starting to get used to it, as frightening as that is. Keeping the windows down seems to help."

"What is it?" Nora asked.

"No idea. The previous owner must have had a serious BO problem. I keep trying to tell myself that a car, any car, even one that's ugly, yellow, and smelly is better than no car at all," I said.

"Speaking as someone who has to walk to and from school in the blistering heat, I can tell you that's definitely true," Nora said.

"Do you live far from here?" I asked.

"Three miles."

"Three *miles*?" I repeated. "You walk that far every day?"

Nora flushed bright red and turned to look out the window, her shoulders hunched defensively.

"I'm sorry. That's just a really long way to go, especially in August. Why doesn't your grandmother drive you?" I asked.

"She can't," Nora said.

"Oh," I said sympathetically. "I'm sorry. Is she disabled?"

Nora laughed. "No way. She plays golf in the morning, and usually goes out shopping with her friends in the afternoons. She says she's too busy to chauffeur me around. I really need to get a bike."

I digested this, trying to imagine my mom or dad requiring me to walk three miles to and from school every day in the late-summer heat, because they couldn't be bothered to pick me up. It wouldn't ever happen. Even my stepmother had dropped me off occasionally in the days before I had a driver's license and a car.

"That stinks," I said.

"Yeah, well, my grandmother was pretty up front about it when I moved here. She told me I could live with her, but I shouldn't expect much from her."

"So why did you move here?" I asked.

"My mom is getting married, and she and her fiancé decided they needed some alone time as newlyweds. My dad's already remarried, but my stepmother isn't all that fond of me," Nora explained.

"I know how that goes," I said.

"You, too? Stepparents are the worst. Anyway, my mom basically dumped me on my grandmother, who's pretty bitter about the whole thing. She keeps telling me she's done raising kids and is entitled to enjoy her retirement," Nora said. I thought Nora sounded pretty bitter herself, but I couldn't blame her. Her parents—and her grandmother—sounded like selfish jerks.

"I'm so sorry," I said. "I sort of know how you feel. My mom moved to London last year, and I was basically forced to move in with my dad and stepmom. Trust me—my stepmom was *not* thrilled with the situation."

"What's your stepmother like?" Nora asked.

I considered this. Peyton and I had never gotten along, but I had to admit, she'd been making more of an effort lately.

"She's not the warmest person you'll ever meet," I said carefully. "But the living situation isn't as bad as I thought it was going to be. It's given me a chance to spend more time with my dad, and I've gotten to know my stepsister better, which has been good. We've gotten pretty close."

Nora nodded. "Well, it's just Gran and me, and she's hardly ever home. I'm usually on my own at the condo, and I think I'm the only one in the building who's under the age of seventy. But at least there's a pool," Nora said.

I hated the idea of Nora sitting alone in an empty apartment without anyone to talk to.

"What are you doing now?" I asked impulsively. "Do you want to come over to my house?"

Nora hesitated, but then finally she shrugged. "Okay. Why not?"

Chapter Seven

When I pulled into the gravel drive of the beach house, there was a familiar red Mini Cooper parked next to Hannah's black SUV.

"What on earth is he doing here?" I muttered.

"What?" Nora asked.

"That's Finn's car," I said. Even if there was another red Mini Cooper out there, it probably didn't have a bumper sticker that read: IF IT WEREN'T FOR PHYSICS AND LAW ENFORCEMENT, I'D BE UNSTOPPABLE.

"That funny guy from school?" Nora asked.

"If by funny you mean the annoying smart-ass, then yes. That's Finn," I said as I turned off the car and opened the door. "I wonder what he's doing here."

"He's probably waiting for you," Nora said as she also got out of the car. She seemed relieved to be away from the stinky smell and out in the fresh air.

"He didn't mention he was coming over," I said.

"Maybe he wanted it to be a surprise."

I shuddered. "That's a truly horrifying thought. The last time Finn tried to surprise me, he did it by posting gossip about me on a Web site."

"Why?" Nora asked.

"Exactly. That is the eternal question when it comes to Finn. *Why?*" I slammed the door shut. "The answer is usually some typically twisted Finn logic that no normal, sane person would ever understand."

"Are you guys together?" Nora asked, as we headed up the walk to the front door.

"Together?" I repeated. "Wait . . . you mean, *together* together? As in dating? You're kidding, right?"

Nora nodded. "Why? He's sort of cute."

"Ugh," I said. "I mean, that would be like dating my brother. If I had a brother. And if that brother spent all of his free time playing disturbing video games." I shook my head and opened the front door. "I'm going to forget you even suggested it."

Nora giggled. It was the first time I'd really heard her laugh. I grinned back at her.

When I opened the front door, Willow was already there waiting for me, her long body wriggling happily.

"Hi, girl. This is Nora," I said, stroking my dog's pretty brindle head.

Nora hesitated, looking warily at Willow. Which was odd. People usually love meeting Willow. She was sweet and beautiful and not even the tiniest bit aggressive. Willow's only enemy was Madonna, Hannah's white puffball of a cat. Every time the two of them got into a tussle, Willow came out on the losing end. She'd had her nose scratched enough times that it made her jumpy to even be in the same room as Madonna.

"I'm not really a dog person," Nora said.

"Don't worry. Willow's really sweet," I said.

Willow stuck out her long nose and sniffed in Nora's direction, but didn't approach her. Instead, the greyhound turned back to me for some more love. I was surprised. Normally, Willow loves to meet new people. I gave her back one last scratch and then said, "Come on. Let's go find out what Finn's up to."

It didn't take long to find him. Finn was sitting at the kitchen table, tapping away on Hannah's laptop, while she—wearing a Bluetooth earpiece—stood behind him, looking over his shoulder. The whole thing was bizarre. Hannah and Finn barely knew each other. And, to make the scene just that much odder, Avery Tallis was perched on one of the tall stools lined up next to the kitchen island.

Avery—who had a thin, pointed face and short, dark hair—used to be at the beach house all the time, back when she and Hannah were best friends. But then Hannah discovered that Avery had stolen an expensive cashmere sweater out of Peyton's closet, and that had—I thought—ended their friendship.

What is Avery doing here now? I wondered.

Avery turned to look at me with narrow, clever eyes, and smiled slyly. Avery didn't like me. It all started when I wouldn't do her math homework for her, and her dislike for me had only grown once I started dating Dex. Avery had wanted to go out with him herself.

"Hi, Miranda. How's life at that weird geek school?" Avery said.

"Just fine, thanks," I said coolly. It was one thing when the kids at my school called it Geek High. It was a joke, an affectionate nickname. It sounded completely different in Avery's sneering tone.

Finn and Hannah looked up from the laptop.

"Hey, M," Finn said. "How's it shaking?"

"It's shaking just fine. What are you doing here, Finn?" I asked.

"He's helping us launch our new Web site. For Match Made," Hannah explained.

"Match Made?" I repeated.

"That's what we're calling the new matchmaking service. You know, it's from that saying 'A match made in heaven.' "

"Or a match made in hell," Finn murmured.

"Don't you like it?" Hannah asked, looking at me anxiously.

"Actually, I really do like it. But who's the *we*? You and Finn?" I asked, hoping, hoping, hoping that wasn't it. The idea of Finn being involved in a matchmaking service was truly horrific. He would see it as a goal—no, not just a goal, but a personal calling—to set up the most hideous, disastrous dates possible, just to amuse himself.

"No, not Finn. He's just helping with the Web site. Avery and I are going to run the business," Hannah said. "Hi. Are you a friend of Miranda's?"

In my shock at finding Avery—not to mention Finn—in our kitchen, I had completely forgotten about Nora. Especially since she'd been so quiet, standing behind me, just inside the kitchen door. Nora looked nervous, her shoulders hunched, one arm wrapped around her torso. It seemed she was trying to take up the smallest amount of space possible.

"Nora, I'm sorry," I said, turning to her. "Come on in and meet everyone. Well, you know Finn. This is my stepsister, Hannah, and this is her"—I hesitated for a beat—"friend Avery Tallis. Everyone, this is Nora Lee."

"Hi," Avery said, flashing Nora the same fake smile she'd given me.

"Nora," Finn said, lifting a fist like a boxer who'd just won a fight.

"Hi," Nora said, raising one hand in a meek wave.

"Are you hungry? Because I'm starving," I asked Nora.

"What a shocker," Hannah said, rolling her eyes. "When it comes to food, Miranda's a bottomless pit."

Ignoring this disparaging comment, I headed to the pantry and began rifling through it. "We have microwave popcorn, or . . . nope, that's about all we have. Oh, wait!" I reached into the back of the cupboard to liberate a bag of tortilla chips. "We also have chips and salsa."

"Yes," Finn said, holding his arms out and waving his hands toward him. "Yes to all of it. Make it happen."

"Actually, I was asking Nora," I told him.

"Nora, you'd like the chips and salsa, *and* the popcorn. And send Miranda out for hot wings, too," Finn said. "Because I think you just might be extra hungry today."

"Finn!" I said, but Nora just giggled and visibly relaxed. *Good old Finn*, I thought. Sometimes his constant wisecracking came in handy. To reward him for putting Nora more at ease, I handed over the chips and salsa to him.

"But don't even think that I'm getting you wings," I said.

•

Nora and I headed to my bedroom with a bowl of freshly popped popcorn. Willow tagged along with us, but Finn stayed with Hannah and Avery to finish work on their Web site.

"Your stepsister is so gorgeous. And she seems really nice, too," Nora said, once we were settled on my bed, the bowl of popcorn between us. Willow sat on my side of the bed, looking hopeful that a spare kernel or two would fall her way.

"Yeah, Hannah's pretty cool," I said. "We used to not get along at all, but since I moved in here, we've gotten pretty close."

"You're lucky," Nora said.

"Are you an only child?" I asked.

She shook her head. "No. I have an older half brother from my mom's first marriage, and two younger half sisters from my dad's third marriage. But I barely know my brother—he chose to live with his dad in Pittsburgh, and only visited us when he had to—and my sisters are practically still babies."

"That sounds complicated," I said.

"I guess you can say my parents aren't very good at commitment," Nora said, her mouth twisting wryly. "Not to each other, or to their kids."

I took a handful of popcorn. Willow stretched out her long neck and sniffed in the direction of my snack. I rolled my eyes but finally relented and dropped a few kernels on the ground for her to snarfle up.

"What's the deal with the other girl?" Nora asked.

"Who? Avery?"

"Yeah. The one who looks like a shark when she smiles."

I laughed. "That's almost exactly what Dex once said about her."

"Dex?"

"My boyfriend," I said, feeling a little self-conscious.

"Does he go to Notting Hill?" Nora asked.

"You really have to start calling it Geek High. Everyone does. Anyway, no, Dex doesn't go to Geek High. In fact, he doesn't even live here anymore. He got a lacrosse scholarship to a prep school in Maine. He just left a few weeks ago, and now we're trying the long-distance thing."

"Hey, me, too," Nora said. "I have a boyfriend back in Boston."

"Really? What his name?" I asked.

I was a little surprised that Nora had a boyfriend. She was so shy, it was hard to imagine her getting up the nerve to talk to a guy, much less go out on a date with one.

"Marcus," Nora said. She sighed. "He's the reason my mom shipped me down here, although she denies it."

"Why? Your mom doesn't like him?"

"She's just a snob. Marcus comes from a pretty rough neighborhood, and he's been living on his own ever since his mom got busted for stealing someone's credit card. He's actually a great guy—very smart, very ambitious—but my mom thinks that anyone who doesn't live in a suburban house with two cars in the driveway is unworthy of her daughter," Nora said. She rolled her eyes in disgust.

"That's really tough," I said sympathetically. "Are you and Marcus staying together?"

"Absolutely," Nora said, lifting her chin. "I love him, and he loves me."

It was the first real spunk I'd seen from Nora. With her eyes glittering and her cheeks flushed with emotion, she looked almost pretty.

"Good for you," I said. "What will your mom say when she finds out you're still together?"

Nora shrugged. "Who knows? I try to avoid talking to her."

We ate some popcorn, and I told Nora about my first assignment for *The Ampersand* and Charlie's advice that I needed to impress my editor.

"I don't know how I'm supposed to write an interesting article about a challenge facing student athletes. Geek High doesn't have any student athletes. So who cares about what problems they face?" I said.

"Does it have to be about a problem?" Nora asked.

"No. Candace—that's the editor—said I could write whatever I want, as long as it has a student-athlete theme. She said I could do an interview or something. But I don't even have anyone I can interview," I said, rubbing my temples in frustration.

"Didn't you just say that your boyfriend is an athlete? Lacrosse, right?" Nora said. "Why don't you interview him?"

I stared at her. It was so obvious. How could I have missed it? Of course I should interview Dex. In fact, he was the perfect person to interview. Instead of a bland, boring jock story, I could write a piece about the ups and downs of moving across the country to attend boarding school on a sports scholarship. And he's from Orange Cove, so it would have a local connection.

"Oh, my gosh. Nora, you're a genius," I said, shaking my head.

Nora giggled. "That's good, considering where I go to high school."

I grinned back at her. "I owe you big," I said. "I can't believe I didn't think of Dex right away."

"Sometimes it helps to bounce story ideas off other people," Nora said modestly. "I used to write for the newspaper at my old school, and we were always helping each other out. By the way, how do you get to be on *The Ampersand* staff? Is there an informational meeting about it?" Nora asked. "I have experience."

I shook my head. "The staff spots for writers are so competitive, they actually have a contest for them in the spring."

Nora's face fell. "That stinks."

"The magazine wins a lot of national awards, so being able to write for it looks really good on college applications. That's why they had to limit how many writers they have each year," I explained. "But if you want, I bet you could work on layout. They're always looking for people to do that."

"Maybe," Nora said without much enthusiasm.

I didn't blame her. Layout seemed incredibly boring to me. I'd much rather create a story than figure out how to fit it onto a page.

"Maybe if you work on layout this year, you'll be more likely to get one of the writer spots next year," I suggested. "The editor in chief is the one who picks who's going to be on the magazine for the upcoming year."

"So basically you're suggesting I shamelessly suck up to her," Nora said.

"Basically," I agreed.

Nora laughed. I liked her like this—relaxed, disarmed. She was nice, I decided. And we had a lot in common—parents who'd let us down, long-distance boyfriends. She stood and went to my window, which looked out on the ocean.

"Your house is amazing," she said. "I can't believe the view."

"Thanks. Although it's not really my house. It's my stepmom's."

"Even so. You're really lucky to live here," Nora said.

"I am?" I said. "I mean, thanks."

It was odd being envied for living here, especially since I'd been horrified when, a year earlier, Sadie had announced she was moving to London and that I'd have to move into the beach house until she returned at some indefinite date in the future. I glanced around the room, trying to look at it with a fresh perspective.

My room—which had once been the guest room—used to be very sterile and white, with low, uncomfortable furniture. But at the end of the summer, in a rare gesture of kindness, Peyton had redecorated it for me. The walls were now a pale blue and there was a thick white shag carpet on the floor. I had a new wrought-iron bed, dressed with a blue and lime green striped comforter, and a black writing desk to work at. I loved the way it had turned out.

"And it must be amazing to be right next to the beach," Nora continued. "I'd be out there all the time."

"Do you want to go out now? Willow needs to go for a walk, anyway," I said.

Nora beamed at me. "Absolutely," she said.

Chapter Eight

Finn was gone by the time I got back from dropping Nora off at her grandmother's condo. Avery was still at the beach house—I could hear her and Hannah in Hannah's room, talking animatedly—so I steered clear of them and headed back to my bedroom. Willow was still there, fast asleep on her round bed, snoring softly.

I texted Dex: SKYPE?

A minute later, my phone chirped with Dex's reply: SURE! GETTING ON NOW.

I opened my laptop and turned on Skype, and a moment later, Dex called.

"Hi," I said excitedly when I saw him.

"Hey, you," Dex said, grinning at me. "What are you up to?"

"I just got back from dropping off my friend Nora. She came over after school."

"Do I know her?"

"No. She just moved here from Boston. She's pretty cool," I said. "How about you?"

"I just got back from afternoon practice," Dex said. He was still wearing his lacrosse shirt and his hair was damp. "Coach had us running intervals all afternoon. I'm beat."

He didn't look tired, though. His pale blue eyes were sparkling and his cheeks were flushed.

He looks happy, I thought. Which was a good thing. I wanted him to be happy.

"Speaking of lacrosse, I need to ask you a favor," I said.

"You need a lacrosse-related favor?" Dex asked, his brow wrinkling with confusion.

"Actually, yes. Yes, I do," I said.

"Wait, let me guess: You've decided to start a girl's lacrosse team at Geek High, and you want me to mentor you," Dex said.

"Like that would ever happen," I said.

"The starting-a-new-team part, or the me-mentoring-you part?"

"Both." I smiled. "I'm so uncoordinated that if I tried running around while carrying a long stick and trying to catch a ball with it, something very bad would happen. Something that would end up with me—and probably half of my teammates—in the hospital. No, I don't want to play lacrosse. I want to interview you for *The Ampersand*."

"Me? Why?"

"I've been assigned to write a piece about student athletes. I thought I could focus the piece on you," I said. Quickly, I added, "It was Nora's idea."

Dex nodded slowly. "Sure. I mean, I'm happy to help out, but I don't know that I'd be all that interesting to your readers. Do they really want to read about our practices and drills and stuff?"

"No, it'll be great. I'll focus on what it's like for you going away to boarding school on an athletic scholarship. You know—how you're adjusting, getting used to a new team," I said.

"Cool," Dex said. "Do you want to interview me now?"

I shook my head. "No, I need to get a list of questions ready first."

"Uh-oh. That sounds a little intimidating. Are you going to ask me hard-hitting questions about where I stand on foreign policy?" Dex teased me.

Before I could respond, though, there was a sudden ruckus on his end of the line. There were some loud whoops, the sound of a door slamming, and then a whole bunch of excited male voices.

"Come on, McConnell. We're tired of waiting for your lazy butt," one of the guys said.

"Yeah, we're starving," another said.

"What's for dinner tonight?" a third asked.

"Meatloaf," someone responded, to a general chorus of groans.

"Let's order pizza instead," someone suggested.

I couldn't tell how many guys were in Dex's dorm room. It sounded like his entire lacrosse team was there, although surely they couldn't all fit. Dex was laughing and trying to keep his friends from grabbing his laptop. One of the guys—blond, pink-cheeked, and square-jawed, with eyebrows and eyelashes so blond, they were practically nonexistent—leaned over Dex's shoulder, and peered at me through the computer screen.

"Who's that?" he asked curiously, as though I were an animal exhibit at a zoo and couldn't understand him. "Is that your girlfriend?"

Wolf whistles ensued, and more of the guys crowded around the screen to look at me. There were shouts of, "Hi, Dex's girlfriend!" Being the object of such frank curiosity caused me to blush bright red, from my toes on up.

"Hi," I said, with a little wave.

"She's pretty cute," one of the guys said, causing my cheeks to grow even hotter.

"She's taken," Dex told him. He smiled wryly at me. "Can I catch you later? It's kind of impossible to talk right now."

"Sure," I said. "Go have dinner."

"See you later," Dex said.

"See you later," I said.

"See you later," some of the guys said.

Dex hung up, and his picture disappeared from my computer screen. I smiled to myself, even though I was feeling a small tug of sadness. I was glad Dex seemed happier, glad he was making friends. And I hadn't really expected him to give up on Brown Academy and transfer back to Orange Cove. Quitting wasn't Dex's style. But, even so, it was hard not to wonder where he and I would end up, once we both accepted that his life was now up there, so far away from Orange Cove.

●

Thankfully, Avery didn't stay for dinner. When I arrived in the kitchen, Peyton and Hannah were seated at the table, while my dad stood at the counter, carving a deli rotisserie chicken.

"Hi, honey," Dad said.

"Hi," I said, taking my seat.

"How was your day, Miranda?" Peyton asked.

I was still having a hard time adjusting to this new Peyton. For most of the time I'd known her, she'd treated me with, at best, cold indifference and, at worst, outright hostility. But her lack of enthusiasm for my presence in the beach house had started to cause a strain in her marriage to my dad. So over the summer, he and Peyton began seeing a marriage counselor. It seemed to be doing them a lot of good—they weren't fighting nearly as much as they used to—and Peyton had been making a real effort to be nicer to me. We'd probably never be close, but as long as we were stuck living together, it was nice to have the hostilities ratcheted down.

"It was fine, thanks," I said politely.

"I was just telling Mom and Richard about my new Web site," Hannah said. She shook her hair back and secured it into a ponytail with an elastic.

"Is it up and running?" I asked.

"It will be soon. Finn said he'd have it ready by the end of the week," Hannah said.

"How did you talk him into doing it for you?" I asked.

"I just asked nicely," Hannah said.

"Hmph," I said.

"What?" she asked.

"Finn doesn't really know what it means to be nice," I warned her. "You'd better double-check your Web site carefully once he's done with it. It wouldn't surprise me if he'd listed himself as the only eligible male for girls to date."

"I thought Finn was still dating Phoebe McCleod," Hannah said.

"He is. But even so, I wouldn't put it past him," I said.

Dad brought the carved chicken to the table.

"Dinner is served," he said, settling the plate down with a flourish.

Along with the chicken, there was pasta tossed with Parmesan cheese and broiled asparagus. I was starving, and loaded up my plate. Hannah rolled her eyes and took about half as much food as I had, while Peyton speared a single asparagus stalk and piece of chicken the size of a half-dollar onto her plate. Peyton almost never ate. This bizarre ability to survive without ever eating was one of the reasons I'd long suspected her of being supernaturally evil.

"Peyton and I have an idea we want to run past you two," Dad said, helping himself to a chicken leg.

"What's that?" Hannah asked.

"We've never been on a family vacation, all four of us together. So we thought that maybe we could take a trip this fall. Maybe drive down to the Keys for a weekend," Dad continued.

"Okay. Fine with me," Hannah said, shrugging.

I was less sure. Even though Peyton had been much nicer to me lately—or, at least, much less hostile—the idea of going on vacation with her didn't exactly thrill me. And I never really thought of Peyton as my family. But my dad looked anxiously over at me, and I didn't want to disappoint him. I knew how important it was to him that we get along.

"Sure. Sounds fun," I said.

And even though it was a lie, my dad's bright smile made me think it was worth it. And who knew? Maybe five hours stuck in a car with Peyton would bring us closer together. It certainly wouldn't kill me.

I glanced over at my stepmother. She was pretending to nibble on the stalk of asparagus without actually letting it pass over her lips. Peyton felt the weight of my stare and she turned her cold, pale eyes on me. They narrowed with dislike.

Yeesh, I thought, as a shiver passed over me. Or maybe five hours in the car together *wouldn't* bring us closer. Maybe it would kill me.

Chapter Nine

"**I**'m not coming to lunch," Charlie announced.

We were standing at our lockers. I'd just stuffed my backpack into my locker and slammed the door shut behind it before any of the random stuff inside—books, notebooks, a spare sweater, a Frisbee that Finn had tossed to me in the hallway last year and I kept forgetting to give back to him—could fall out.

"What do you mean, you're not coming to lunch?" I asked, turning to her in surprise. Charlie's cheeks were flushed, and she was rocking back and forth from her toes to her heels. Charlie was manic-depressive, and this sort of nervous energy was always a sign that she was entering into a manic phase. "You have to eat."

"I'm not hungry," Charlie said. "And I want to paint."

"You have an art period after lunch. Paint then," I said.

"No, I want to work straight through."

"Why?" I asked.

"Because I had an epiphany last night," Charlie announced. "At Grounded."

"You had an epiphany at the coffee shop?"

"Yes, why?"

"It just doesn't seem like the sort of place you'd go to have a spiritual realization," I said.

"I didn't go there in order to have a spiritual realization. I went there to have a decaf latte and do my physics homework," Charlie said. "But then I ran into Finn."

"Really? He must have gone there straight from my house," I said. "Funny he didn't mention it. But, then, he was probably too busy scarfing down pizza. He had a large pepperoni pizza delivered to the beach house, and ate the whole thing himself."

Charlie looked at me. "Wait. Why was Finn ordering pizza to your house yesterday?"

"He was there helping Hannah set up a Web site for her new matchmaking business. Don't ask."

"No, I think I'm going to need more details about that," Charlie said.

"We'll get back to it. First, tell me about your epiphany. And hurry. I'm starving," I said.

"Okay. So Finn came in and sat at my table, and we actually had a really good talk."

I gave a disbelieving snort. When Finn and Charlie were together, he tormented her and she insulted him. It was probably the main reason they'd never gotten together.

"No, really. We actually talked. A real conversation. It was nice for a change," Charlie said.

I leaned against my locker. "What did you talk about? Did you tell him how you feel about him?"

"Of course not," Charlie said, dismissively waving one hand. "Finn was telling me about a book he's been reading called *The Art of War*. It was written by some military genius two thousand years ago, and is apparently still the definitive treatise on battlefield strategies."

"I don't think Finn should be allowed to read books on strategic warfare. It can't lead to anything good," I said.

"I would normally agree, but it was actually really interesting. And Finn was so normal when he was talking to me about it. And I don't even mean normal for him. I mean he was acting like a normal person in general. He even bought me a coffee, which he never does. It was almost like we were—" Charlie stopped abruptly and pressed her lips together.

"It was almost like you were on a date?" I asked sympathetically.

Charlie gave a half nod and a shrug, which I took as a big yes.

"So, what happened?"

"Phoebe showed up. She and Finn had plans, which he had, of course, neglected to tell me," Charlie said. Her eyes darkened.

"I'm sorry," I said, patting her arm sympathetically.

Charlie shrugged again. "When Phoebe saw Finn and me sitting there together, she came rushing over and made a big show of sitting on Finn's lap and playing kissy face with him." Charlie demonstrated, puckering her lips in a way that was more fishlike than kisslike. "The whole thing was so revolting, I had to leave immediately. Anyway, that's when I had my epiphany."

"Which was?" I asked. My stomach gave a low rumble. I wished we were having this conversation over lunch—even a mediocre Geek High lunch—rather than standing in the school corridor.

"Instead of just sitting around waiting for Finn to realize that he has feelings for me, I should use the feelings I have for him in my artwork," Charlie said. "I'm going to do a whole series of paintings fleshing out all of the pain and longing that's caused by unrequited love. It's going to be very modern, very ethereal, very Chagall-inspired. I've already sketched out the first one."

She reached into her bag, pulled out a sheet of paper, and thrust it at me. On it was a pencil-drawn sketch of a girl—at least, I think it was a girl; it was a tall figure with long hair blowing behind her—with her arms wrapped around a heart. Not a heart shape, but an actual heart with lots of valves. Behind the girl, in the far-off distance, a tidal wave was swelling.

"Very cool," I said, handing the drawing back. "Except for the heart. That's kind of gross."

"I was going to do a heart shape, but that seemed too literal. I want it to be gritty, so I used a pig's heart instead," Charlie explained.

"So is this girl supposed to be you?" I asked.

"Not necessarily. She represents all intelligent women who are overlooked in favor of dimbos," Charlie said. She hoisted her book bag over one shoulder. "Anyway, I have to go. I need to start painting while I'm feeling inspired."

"Good luck," I said.

Charlie flashed me a pained smile. "Thanks. Sorry I'm ditching you for lunch."

"No worries," I said.

Charlie hurried off in the direction of the art room. I watched her go, wondering whether her new obsession with unrequited love was something I should worry about, before deciding that it was probably a good thing for her to express herself. Even if it was with pictures of pig hearts.

I headed toward the cafeteria, my spirits drooping a bit. Charlie and I always ate lunch together. Sure, I had other friends at school, and could definitely find someone to eat with. But it was always awkward to stand in the doorway of the cafeteria, looking around for a spare seat while feeling like a complete loser.

"Hi, Miranda," Nora said, suddenly appearing beside me. "Are you going to lunch?"

"Yes," I said. "You, too?"

Nora nodded. "Do you mind if I eat with you?" she asked shyly.

"Sounds great," I said. I smiled at Nora. "Hey, I have the same top."

I hadn't noticed Nora's blue plaid halter top with white buttons down the front when we were in lit class. I'd bought the identical shirt at the Gap when Hannah took me back-to-school shopping. I hadn't been at all sure about the shirt—halter tops made me nervous; it seemed like there were too many things that could go wrong with them—but when I'd worn it to school a few days earlier, I'd gotten lots of compliments on it. Even better, horrible Felicity Glen had given me the stink eye, which meant that it must have looked really good on me.

"You do?" Nora asked.

"Yep. The Gap, right?"

"That's right. We must have the same taste," Nora said.

"Or, more accurately, you and my stepsister have the same taste," I said. "She's the one who picked it out. Anyway, it looks cute on you. Although you should put on a cardigan, or you're going to get busted on a dress-code violation."

Nora did look nice. She was wearing the shirt over a pair of crisp white shorts and navy blue grosgrain flip-flops. She looked much more like a Florida girl than she had on the first day of school, when she'd shown up in dark clothes and Doc Martens.

"I have a cardigan in my bag," Nora said. We stopped for a moment while she dug out the white cardigan and put it on. "What happens if you get a dress-code violation?"

"Nothing really. Just a warning and a hassle about it from the headmaster," I said.

When we got to the cafeteria, Nora and I found a couple of empty seats at one of the corner tables. Platters of sandwiches, fruit salad, and peanut butter cookies were already out on the table.

"It's so weird that the food here is served this way," Nora said, helping herself to a sandwich and a bunch of red grapes. "My old school had an actual cafeteria, with food that was spooned out onto plastic trays by grim women wearing hairnets."

"They have a whole theory behind it," I explained. "Apparently, they think if they put the food out on the tables, family style, it will foster a sense of camaraderie among the students."

"That sounds totally bogus," Nora said.

"Yeah, I'm sure some school administrator just made it up. All it does is create a free-for-all with everyone trying to grab the best sandwiches," I agreed.

"I had fun yesterday hanging out at your house," Nora said.

"Me, too," I said. After Nora and I had eaten the rest of our popcorn, we'd taken Willow on a long walk down the beach. Even though Nora still didn't seem all that comfortable around Willow, she at least stopped flinching and gasping every time Willow sniffed in her direction. I kept assuring Nora that Willow was very gentle and not at all aggressive, and Nora had finally seemed more relaxed around my greyhound by the time we got back to the beach house.

"And I think I'm going to take your advice and work on layout for *The Ampersand*," Nora said.

"Good! I know they're always looking for people. And your experience will be a big plus," I said.

"Did you get any work done on your article?"

"No. But I did talk to Dex about it, and he agreed to let me interview him. I just wanted some time to think about what questions I'm going to ask. Besides, some of his friends came in while we were talking, so Dex had to get off."

"That's too bad," Nora said sympathetically. "The long-distance-dating thing is so hard."

"Did you talk to Marcus last night?" I asked.

Nora nodded. "He wasn't very talkative, though. I couldn't tell if he was just feeling quiet or if he was actually upset about something. It's so hard not being there and seeing him in person."

"Have you tried talking to him on Skype?" I asked. "That way you could at least see him. That's how Dex and I talk most of the time."

"Marcus doesn't have a computer," Nora said.

"Really?" I asked. This surprised me. Everyone I knew had a computer. In fact, laptops were mandatory for all Geek High students. Then I remembered what Nora had said about Marcus being poor, and that was at least part of the reason why her mother was against their relationship. "Maybe he could use one at school or borrow a friend's?"

"Maybe," Nora said, with a shrug. She didn't seem all that keen on the idea, so I decided to drop it.

"Did you ask him if he was upset about something?" I asked instead.

"Yeah. He said he wasn't. But who knows? I'm so far away, I can't tell what's really going on with him," Nora said. She sighed and dropped her half-eaten ham sandwich on her plate. I didn't blame her—lunch was especially bad that day. The sandwiches tasted as if they were about two weeks old, and the apple slices were mealy and covered with brown spots.

"Yeah, I know what you mean. Dex has this whole other life up at his school that I'll never be part of," I said, pushing aside my plate. "And it's good that he has a life there—I want him to—but at the same time, it makes me feel even farther away from him."

"I know exactly what you mean. I feel bad sometimes, because I want Marcus to be happy, of course . . . but I also sort of want him to be miserable, too, because I'm not there. You know?"

"Yes!" I said, nodding. "In fact, just the other day, Dex was feeling homesick, and said that he was thinking about transferring back to Orange Cove High. And even though I knew it wouldn't be the right thing to do—this school is such a great opportunity for him, and he really hasn't been there long enough to give up on it—I couldn't help feeling a little . . ." I trailed off.

"Happy that he was unhappy?" Nora suggested.

I nodded, feeling guilty admitting it. "That's pretty awful, isn't it?"

"No, not at all. I totally understand. I feel the same way."

"You do?" I asked. It was such a relief to have someone to talk to about this. Someone who knew exactly what I was going through. Not even Charlie or Hannah would get it, since neither of them had ever had a long-distance relationship. Charlie would probably tell me that I had to trust Dex, and Hannah would give me terrible advice about how I should try to make Dex jealous to keep him interested. But Nora knew what it was really like. She understood where I was coming from.

"What do people do on dates around here?" Nora asked. She smiled wryly. "Or, should I say, what did you do when Dex was still here?"

"The usual stuff. Movies, dinner, going to the beach," I said. "Is that what you did in Boston?"

"Pretty much, minus going to the beach. Is there someplace cool to hang out around here?" Nora asked.

She spent the rest of lunch asking me a lot of questions about Geek High and life in Orange Cove, and who my friends were, and what various kids at school were like. After what seemed like the hundredth question, I finally laughed.

"I can tell you were a reporter. I feel like I'm being interviewed," I said.

Nora blushed, and looked down at the table.

"Sorry. I guess I've been asking too many questions," she said sheepishly.

"No, it's fine," I said, realizing that I shouldn't tease Nora the way I would Charlie or Finn. She was so shy.

"I just . . ." Nora began, but then stopped, and blushed an even deeper shade of red. In fact, she flushed right down her neck and into the V of her plaid halter top.

"You want to fit in?" I suggested. She nodded. "Yeah, I totally get that. Don't worry. Ask me whatever you want."

"Thanks, Miranda," Nora said. She looked up at me shyly. "You're a really good friend."

Chapter Ten

The following Saturday, Charlie and I made plans to go to the beach. I was really looking forward to hanging out with Charlie. She'd been spending all of her time immersed in her new art project, and I had barely seen her outside of class all week. I was happy that she'd found a way to channel her unhappiness over the situation with Finn, but I really missed having her around to talk to.

Our plan was that she was going to arrive at the beach house at ten in the morning, and then we'd bring a picnic with us down to the beach. I already had the cooler packed with all of our favorites: Fluffernutter sandwiches, salt and vinegar potato chips, green apples, and, for dessert, chocolate-covered graham crackers, along with enough bottled water to keep us hydrated for a week in the middle of a desert. Which was exactly how hot Florida in the late summer felt.

Five minutes before she was due to arrive, Charlie called.

"Hi! Are you on your way over?" I asked.

"Actually . . . no. I'm sorry, Miranda, but I can't come over today after all," she said.

"What? Why not?" I asked.

"I've been up all night painting, and I'm having one of the most productive sessions I've ever had. Can't stop now," Charlie said. "I don't want to interrupt the creative flow."

She was talking very fast. Charlie's bipolar disorder caused her to swing between periods such as this—when she sounded and acted as though she'd been guzzling shots of espresso—and periods where she could barely get out of bed.

"Okay, if that's what you want to do," I said, not able to keep the disappointment out of my voice.

"It's not what I want to do. It's what I *have* to do," Charlie said. "Doesn't this ever happen to you when you're writing? Aren't there times when there are so many ideas inside of you, you feel like you're going to burst if you don't get them out?"

"Yeah, I guess," I admitted.

Charlie paused. "Are you mad at me?" she asked.

"No, it's okay. I understand," I said.

"Thanks, Miranda," Charlie said. "I'll make it up to you."

After we hung up, I considered the cooler, which was sitting on the counter. It seemed a shame to waste a perfectly good picnic. *If Dex were home, he'd have come over*, I thought with a pang. We'd spent a good part of the summer at the beach together, sitting side by side in the hot sun, watching for dolphins. Or, while Dex surfed, I would sit under the shade of a big striped umbrella and work on my short stories, looking up periodically to watch him ride a wave in.

I gave myself a mental shake. There was no point in wallowing over Dex's absence. It just made it even worse. I padded out of the kitchen and headed to Hannah's room.

I knocked on her door. "Hannah?"

"Come in," Hannah said.

She was sitting at her curvy white vanity, examining her skin in a magnified mirror. Her hair was caught back in a stubby ponytail, and she was wearing a red, kimono-style bathrobe.

"What are you doing?" I asked.

"Trying to figure out what's going on with my pores," Hannah said.

"What's wrong with them?" I asked.

"They're huge," Hannah said.

"That's probably because you're looking in a magnified mirror. That makes everything look larger," I suggested.

Hannah gave me a withering look. "I know how the mirror works. But, seriously, look at my pores. Aren't they gross?"

I peered at Hannah's face. I couldn't see what she was talking about. Her pores—which were barely noticeable—looked completely normal. In fact, Hannah had beautiful skin. I'd never even seen her get a zit.

"No. Your pores look fine to me," I said.

Hannah sighed and shook her head at my ignorance. "I'm going to put on a refining mask. And then I'll exfoliate. Maybe that will help," she said.

"Yeah, sure," I said. "Anyway, do you want to go to the beach with me? I packed a picnic lunch. We can hang out, catch up. I'll even let you explain eyeliner to me."

A lot had changed since I'd moved into the beach house. A year ago, I would never have invited my stepsister to go anywhere with me. But over time, we'd actually become friends. It would be fun to hang out with Hannah for the day, even if it did mean I'd almost certainly have to suffer through further discussions of the size of her pores.

"Explain eyeliner? What is there to explain?" Hannah asked.

"I don't get it. How do you put it on without sticking the pencil in your eye? And how do you manage to draw a straight line? Every time I try, it turns out wonky," I said.

"Okay, this is a serious problem that we have to address. But not today. Not while I'm in the middle of a complexion crisis," Hannah said.

"You could do the mask and exfoliator thingy when we get back," I suggested.

"No. Sorry, Miranda, but this is going to take all of my energy and concentration for the rest of the day," Hannah said, shaking her head regretfully. "I can't risk getting an oily T-zone."

Hannah picked up her mirror and went back to staring at her pores. I sighed and left her to it.

I headed to my room, wondering what I was going to do with my day. Willow was there, sleeping on her round bed. When I walked in, she opened one amber eye, looked at me, then closed it again and went back to sleep. So much for canine companionship. I flopped on my bed, wondering whether I should call Finn, but then remembered that he didn't like hanging out at the beach. He claimed that sand always ended up in places on his body where sand should never be. And, anyway, Finn would almost certainly be planning to spend the day in a darkened room, playing violent video games and eating Pop-Tarts straight from the box.

I need to find some new friends, I thought.

Then I had a sudden flash of brilliance. *Nora*.

I called Nora on her cell phone. She answered immediately.

"Hey, it's Miranda," I said. "What are you up to?"

"I'm sitting on the balcony of my grandmother's apartment, watching a group of seventy-year-old women perform water aerobics in the pool. Or, in other words, absolutely nothing," Nora said. "Why? What did you have in mind?"

"Do you want to come over? I made a picnic, and I thought we could take it down to the beach," I said.

"I'd love to," Nora said.

"I'll come pick you up," I offered.

"That would be great. Thanks," Nora said, and I thought I could hear a smile in her voice.

•

It was yet another hot, humid day. A faint breeze blew off the water, which helped somewhat, although the sand was as hot as an oven. Nora and I were side by side on an old blanket, smeared with high-SPF sunscreen to keep us from turning lobster red.

"Have you ever surfed?" Nora asked. She was sitting back, propped up on her elbows, watching the surfers riding the rolling waves. I had to keep reminding myself not to look for Dex out among them.

I snorted. "No way. I'm such a klutz, I can barely stand up on solid ground."

Nora laughed. "I'm the same way. I'd probably kill myself out there. Or get eaten by a shark."

"Dex surfs," I said. "He parasurfs, too."

"What's that?"

"It's surfing with a big, overhead parachute that lifts you off the water. It's really hard, but he's great at it," I said proudly.

"Wow," Nora said admiringly. "I've always wanted to date a surfer. Those guys are really cute."

I followed her gaze, taking in the various guys riding waves toward shore. I recognized a few of them from hanging out at the beach with Dex. For the most part, they were a bunch of goofs.

"You think?" I asked.

"Absolutely," Nora said.

"Does Marcus surf?"

"I don't think Marcus knows what a surfboard is," Nora said. She pushed her sunglasses back on her head and narrowed her eyes as she considered the surfers. "Do you know the guy in the orange board shorts?"

I squinted at the distant surfer. "I think that's Colby Jenkins. I can't tell for sure, though. He's too far away."

"Do you know him?"

"We were in the same class before I transferred to Geek Middle," I said. "But we were never really friends. I think Dex used to surf with him from time to time."

"He's really cute," Nora said. "I wonder if he has a girlfriend?"

I glanced at her. "What about Marcus?"

"What? Oh . . . Marcus. Well. Who knows what will happen with him?" Nora asked. She seemed flustered, and quickly pulled her sunglasses back on.

I remembered what Nora had said about Marcus being uncommunicative when they'd talked on the phone a few days earlier, and wondered if things had gotten worse since then.

"The long-distance thing is hard," I said sympathetically. "My stepsister keeps telling me that most high school couples break up when they go to college."

"Yeah, I've heard that, too. But Marcus and I are fine. For now," she added.

I had the feeling that something really was wrong, but Nora didn't seem as though she wanted to talk about it. I decided I should probably change the subject.

"Have you done the physics homework yet?" I asked.

"I started it, but it's really hard," Nora said.

"That's what I thought, too. Finn is oddly good at physics, even though he basically never studies," I said. "Maybe we can get him to help us with it. Although this is Finn we're talking about, so we'll have to bribe him."

"With what?" Nora asked.

"I don't know. Maybe a new comic book. Or a promise to help on a future prank. Finn loves pranks."

"You mean like putting Saran Wrap on a toilet seat, or putting sugar in a salt shaker?" Nora asked.

"No. He works on a much larger scale. Finn's not truly happy unless the Secret Service is called in to investigate," I said. "On second thought, maybe I should just stick with the comic book idea."

"Yeah. I don't want to end up with a criminal record just to get a good grade in physics," Nora said.

"Very sensible," I agreed, tipping my face back and closing my eyes against the bright sun.

"So, tell me more about Finn," Nora said.

"Finn? What do you want to know?"

"What's he like?"

I considered this. "He jokes around a lot. Finn's almost never serious about anything. And he's really into computer games. He plays them constantly. Oh, and he's developed a few games, too, all of which were huge sellers."

Nora was obviously impressed. She pushed her sunglasses back on her head again and looked at me. "Are you serious?"

I nodded "Finn's really talented. Most of the kids at Geek High are. Of course, he also has appalling judgment and is dating this complete ditz who goes to Orange Cove High, for no other reason than the fact that she's pretty and she'll talk to him," I said.

I reached into the cooler and pulled out an icy-cold bottle of water, twisted off the cap, and took a sip.

"Does Finn know your friend Charlie likes him?" Nora asked.

I started, which caused me to pour water straight down the top of my bathing suit.

"Ack!" I said as the cold water hit my sun-warmed skin.

Nora handed me a towel, which I used to mop up the spilled water.

"How did you know about that?" I asked.

"It's pretty obvious. I could tell from the way she looks at him," Nora said.

"Really?" I asked. I knew Charlie would not be happy to hear that. Not that I had any intention of telling her.

Nora nodded. "Yeah. I'm surprised he hasn't noticed."

"I'm not. For such a smart guy, Finn can be completely clueless," I said. I leaned back on my elbows again. Now that the initial shock of the cold water had passed, it actually felt pretty good to cool off. I eyed the water, wondering if it was time for a dip.

"What's Charlie like?" Nora asked.

"Charlie? She's amazing. She's smart and funny and a really talented painter. You should see her work," I said. "Lately, she's been painting on these huge canvases. They're pretty cool."

"I like her hair," Nora said.

"Yeah, she always has it dyed some wacky color," I said. "She changes it so often, I can never even remember what the color of the day is."

"Have you been friends for a long time?"

"Four years. Ever since seventh grade, when I transferred to Geek Middle. I met Charlie on my first day of school, and we've been best friends pretty much ever since," I said.

"That's cool," Nora said, and I thought she sounded a little wistful.

"Do you have close friends back home in Boston?" I asked.

"Yeah, I had a pretty tight group of friends. And we still text and stuff. But I feel so far away from everyone now," Nora said. She sat up, hunching her shoulders, and dug her toes into the sand.

"This whole move has been really hard on you, huh?" I said sympathetically.

Nora smiled ruefully. "I'm sorry. You're probably tired of hearing me complain about it. I'm tired of hearing me complain about it."

I shook my head. "Not at all. But I'll tell you what—let's just have a really fun day today. Maybe Orange Cove will start to grow on you."

"It's already growing on me. I just have to get used to how hot it is down here," Nora said.

"Do you want to go for a swim?" I asked, standing and dusting the sand off my bottom.

"Sure," Nora said, standing, too. She hesitated. "Um . . . there aren't any sharks in the water, are there?"

"I'm sure there are somewhere. It is the ocean, after all. But maybe we'll get lucky and they'll leave us alone," I said cheerfully. Then, seeing how round Nora's eyes had gone, I laughed. "I'm kidding. Come on—it'll be fine. I promise."

Chapter Eleven

Nora accompanied me to the next *Ampersand* meeting. She'd already spoken to Candace about joining the layout staff, and reported back that Candace had welcomed her on board.

Nora and I shared a table in the *Ampersand* office, while Candace—today wearing a crisp navy blue shirt dress cinched at the waist with a leather belt, her straight, blue-black hair gleaming under the fluorescent overhead lights—stood and called the meeting to order.

"Okay, everyone settle down," Candace called out. The chatter and laughter immediately died down. Candace had that effect on people. "First, I want to get a status update from everyone." She consulted her notepad. "Peter, Coleen, how's the SAT prep course article coming?"

I felt a thrill of horror. I hadn't started working on my article yet. It wasn't due for another week, so I'd thought I had plenty of time. Apparently not. And now I was going to have to think of something to say in front of everyone. My stomach gave a nervous lurch. It didn't help when Coleen and Peter gave long, detailed reports of the many interviews they'd already conducted for their pieces.

Nora scribbled something on a piece of paper and pushed it across the table to me. I looked down at it.

The note read: *Have you written your article?*

I wrote, *No* underneath, underlined it three times, and pushed it back toward her.

Nora looked at the note and let out a faint snort of laughter. She wrote back, *Eek!* I giggled.

"Miranda, do you have something you'd like to share with the rest of us?"

I started and looked up. The entire *Ampersand* staff had turned to stare at me. Heat flooded my cheeks. I had a sudden horrific image of Candace seizing the note Nora and I were passing, and reading out loud my admission that I hadn't made any progress on my student-athlete piece. But when I glanced down, I saw Nora surreptitiously sliding the paper into her backpack.

"Um, no, thanks. I'm good," I said.

Candace continued to stare at me. Her eyes were a clear, piercing blue.

"What about your student-athlete article?" Candace said.

"Oh, right. Sorry. I've, um, decided to interview a local lacrosse player who received a sports scholarship to attend a prep school in the Northeast this year. I'm going to write about his experience going away to school," I said.

Candace nodded. "That sounds like an interesting angle. Have you done the interview?"

"It's scheduled for this evening," I said. Which was sort of true. Dex and I had a date to talk on Skype that night, so I could totally do the interview then.

"Good. I look forward to reading it," Candace said. "Tabitha, how is your short story coming?"

Nora gave me a thumbs-up under the table. I exhaled deeply, relieved that the group's attention was no longer on me.

•

After the meeting, Nora and I walked out together. I was giving her a ride home.

"Howdy," a familiar voice called out.

I turned to see Finn walking down the hall toward us. He was looking jaunty in blue plaid shorts and a T-shirt emblazoned with the slogan HIPPIES SMELL.

"How did you get that past the headmaster?" I asked, pointing at his T-shirt.

"Headmaster Hughes? He laughed when he saw it," Finn said, joining us. "I think he agrees with the sentiment."

"Typical. You get away with everything," I said.

"Where's Charlie been hiding? I've barely seen her in days," Finn said.

"She's been busy painting," I said vaguely.

"Busy painting, huh? So you've decided to replace her with Nora here?" Finn asked.

"Excuse me?" I said.

"Is Nora your replacement Charlie? I've noticed the two of you have been spending a lot of time together. Are you new BFFs?" Finn asked.

I rolled my eyes at Nora, and she grinned back at me.

"Come on, Nora. It's time to put the Let's Ignore Finn plan into action," I said.

Nora and I continued to walk down the hallway. Undaunted, Finn joined us.

"If you keep spending so much time together, we're going to have to merge your names, like Bennifer or Brangelina. Mirora? No, that doesn't sound right. Noranda? That's not good, either. It would be a lot easier if you could change your name to Brad or Ben, Nora. Then you could be Biranda," Finn said.

"I sort of like Mirora. It sounds like the name of a high priestess," Nora mused.

"But Noranda sounds like a prescription skin cream," Finn remarked. "The kind that zaps zits or hemorrhoids."

"Or, we could just keep our regular names," I suggested.

"You're no fun. So, where are we heading?" Finn asked.

"Out to Miranda's car," Nora said. "Or, as I've decided to rename it, the Stinkmobile."

Finn laughed appreciatively. I was momentarily taken aback. I think it was the first time I'd ever heard Nora make a joke.

"Classic," Finn said. "That car needs to be fumigated."

"I took it to the car wash this weekend and had them pipe in a deodorizing fragrance," I said.

"I love that stuff. What did you get? New-car smell? That's my favorite," Finn said. "If I could, I'd go around smelling like a new car. I wish they'd make it into a cologne. Do you think someone sells that?"

"No," I said.

"Note to self: invent a cologne with new-car smell," Finn said.

"What fragrance did you really get?" Nora asked.

"Strawberry-banana," I said. "I thought it sounded nice and fruity."

"Did it work on the stink?"

"Not really," I said sadly. "The stink is still there, only now with an undertone of artificial strawberry-banana smell. Which, I have to say, is really not much of an improvement."

"Awesome," Finn said with relish.

"I told Miranda she could market the smell as a weapon. Find a way to get it into an atomizer, and then spray it at a mugger or something. It would work better than pepper spray," Nora said, to Finn's growing hilarity.

What? She's never said that to me, I thought.

"That's brilliant," Finn said. "And then the cops would have an easy time tracking down the bad guy. All they'd have to do is follow the odor."

Nora giggled appreciatively.

"Thanks, guys. That's just so helpful," I said dryly. "No, never mind me. I'll just suffer with my stinky car while you two laugh at me."

"Oh, come on, M," Finn said. He threw one arm around my neck and another around Nora's. "We kid because we love."

"And because we really want you to do something about the stink. Seriously, it's so bad that whenever I'm in your car, I want to stick my head out the window like a dog," Nora said.

"Ha, ha," I said as Nora and Finn cracked up. "Don't forget, without me, you'd be walking home, Nora."

"No, she wouldn't. I'd drive you home, Nora," Finn said.

"Aw, thanks, Finn," Nora said.

"Wait, no, I take it back. I wouldn't drive you home. I'm meeting Phoebe at Grounded," Finn said. "By the way, M, tell Hannah I got her Web site up and running today during calculus class."

"During class? Didn't Mr. Gordon notice?"

"Dunno," Finn said. "I had on my headphones, so I couldn't really hear what he was saying."

I rolled my eyes, while Nora snickered. She seemed to think he was kidding. I was pretty sure he wasn't.

"Let me know what Hannah says when she sees it," Finn said.

There was something in his tone—and, when I turned sharply to look up at him, a mischievous glint in his dark eyes—that told me he was up to something.

"What did you do?" I asked.

"Whatever do you mean?" Finn asked, feigning innocence. Another bad sign.

"Seriously. What did you do to Hannah's Web site?" I asked.

Finn looked wounded. "I help out your stepsister, generously giving up an entire calculus period, during which I could have been mastering the tenth level of *Staroids*, and this is the sort of thanks I get? Accusations of skullduggery? I'm wounded, Miranda. Truly, I'm deeply hurt."

"No, you're not," I said.

"Yeah, you're right. I'm not," Finn agreed.

"What's *Staroids*?" Nora asked.

"It's a totally rad game. It combines the best elements of an RPG and a first-person shooter. It's brilliantly violent. I can't believe I didn't come up with it," Finn enthused.

"I love video games," Nora said.

"You do?" Finn asked. He looked at me, his brow furrowed. "Why have you been hiding this from me, Miranda? You know the rules. All gaming enthusiasts are to be brought to my attention immediately."

"I didn't know," I said. In fact, in all of the conversations I'd had with Nora, she'd never once mentioned video games.

I suddenly had a worrying thought. Was Nora joking around with Finn and pretending to be interested in video games because she was romantically interested in him? I sincerely hoped not. It was bad enough that Charlie was suffering from her unrequited love for Finn. I didn't want to lose another friend to his inexplicable charms.

Chapter Twelve

That night, after dinner, I sat down at my desk and came up with a list of questions to ask Dex. It was the first time I'd ever interviewed anyone, and I was feeling a little nervous about it.

At seven o'clock, I was in front of my laptop, ready for Dex's call. He was always very prompt. But as I sat there, staring at the Skype site, waiting for it to ring . . . it didn't: 7:03 . . . 7:07 . . . 7:09. By 7:12, I was starting to get annoyed. Had Dex forgotten? Or was he too busy to call? No, it couldn't be that he was too busy—he would at least have texted me to let me know he couldn't talk.

I considered turning Skype and my cell phone off, so that if Dex called, he wouldn't be able to get a hold of me. But, no, that would be petty and immature, and, besides, I really did need to interview him. Also, I wanted to hear about his first official day of school. I wondered whether I should text him to remind him of our phone date, but just as I was reaching for my phone, Skype started to ring.

"Sorry I'm late," Dex said as soon as we were connected. "Practice ran over, and then I had to get dinner before the dining hall closed. I swear, I have never eaten faster in my life, and when I was done, I ran all the way back to my dorm."

He looked flushed and out of breath. All of my irritation vanished, replaced by a soft glow of delight. He hadn't forgotten about me. He'd run home to talk to me.

"Don't worry; it's fine," I told him.

"How are you doing?" Dex asked, smiling warmly in the way that always caused a zing to shoot through me.

"I'm great. How was your first day of classes?"

Dex's smile slipped away. "So unbelievably hard. You wouldn't believe how tough the classes are here. Actually, maybe you would—that's probably what you're used to at Geek High. But I had no idea it was going to be so intense. I'm going to be up half the night trying to get all of my homework done." Dex ran one hand through his red hair. "I'm probably going to be the dumbest kid in class."

"Oh, please," I said. "You always get really good grades."

"At Orange Cove High. Seriously, this place is on an entirely different level. I don't know if I'll be able to keep up," Dex said. He did look really stressed out. His face was pale and drawn.

"I'm sure you'll do fine," I said. I hesitated. As much as I wanted to interview Dex, I didn't want to monopolize his time, especially if he was feeling stressed about his workload. "Do you have to go now, so you can do your homework?"

"No, I don't want to hang up yet," Dex said quickly.

"Would you mind if I interviewed you for my article? Or is this a bad time?"

"Sure, go ahead," Dex said.

"Are you sure? It's just that my editor is leaning on me to get it done," I said apologetically.

"Ask away. My life is an open book," Dex said. He grinned at me, looking more like himself. "And to answer your first question, no, I don't have any special beauty secrets. I'm just naturally this good-looking."

I rolled my eyes. "Yeah, like that's going in the article. Okay, first question: why did you decide to go to Brown Academy?"

"They offered me a full scholarship. And it's a really good school and has a great lacrosse program. A lot of the top college teams recruit here," Dex said.

I scribbled down his answer in my notebook.

"Was it hard to make the decision to leave home and go away to school?" I asked.

"Yes," Dex said, his voice soft. "Very hard."

I looked at him. "Care to elaborate?" I asked.

Dex laughed. "Are you just trying to get me to tell you how much I miss you?"

"No! Think of me as a professional reporter," I protested.

"Okay. Yes, it's really hard being away from my family and friends. And it's especially hard being away from my girlfriend," Dex said.

I wrote it down, trying to ignore the fact that my insides were turning warm and gooey. I had to stay on task, or I'd get another lecture from Candace.

I asked Dex some more questions, covering how his family had reacted to his getting into such a good prep school, what it was like being the new guy on his lacrosse team, what the team's training regimen was like, what a typical day at prep school was like, and what he was looking forward to when lacrosse season began in the spring. Dex gave me great answers, and I started to feel more confident that my article was shaping up to be pretty interesting. How great would it be if I ended up impressing Candace with my very first piece?

"Anything else?" Dex asked.

I checked my list.

"One more, and I think we're done. How are you adjusting to your new school?" I asked.

"Pretty well, I think. The guys on the team are all pretty cool. And the campus is really nice. I don't know how I'm going to handle the winter—I've never even seen snow in person before—but since I may end up failing out before then, I guess I shouldn't worry about it now," Dex said.

"You are not going to fail out," I said, forgetting for a moment that I was supposed to be conducting an interview. "You'll be fine."

"A girl in my history class is forming a study group. She asked me if I wanted to join," Dex said.

Jealousy hit me like a glowing green laser ray. A girl? What girl? I mean, obviously I knew there were girls at his school. Whom he would at some point speak to. But even so . . . the idea of him hanging out with those girls, joining a study group, smiling his amazing smile at them . . .

"Miranda?" Dex asked. "Are you okay? You're not saying anything."

"What? Oh, no. I'm fine," I said quickly. "Just thinking about my article."

I didn't want him to know that I was jealous. And, besides, I trusted Dex. I'd spent the whole summer worrying that he was going to fall back in love with his ex-girlfriend, Wendy—who was stunning and, unfortunately, too nice to hate—and it turned out that he wasn't at all interested in her. So I knew I shouldn't let my imagination run wild. It would just make me miserable.

My door opened with an explosive bang. I jumped in my seat and turned to see my stepsister storming into my bedroom. Hannah's cheeks were flushed and her eyes were slitted with anger.

"You will not believe what your friend Finn did to my Web site!" Hannah announced. She strode across the room and towered over me. "Look at it right now. Matchmade.com. Go on."

"Hannah, I'm sort of right in the middle of something," I said, gesturing toward Dex's face on my computer screen.

"Oh, hey, Dex. I didn't see you there," Hannah said.

"Hi, Hannah. How's it going?" Dex asked.

"I'm in the middle of a crisis. I need Miranda," Hannah announced.

"Can this possibly wait?" I asked.

"No," Hannah said, with a firm shake of her head that sent her pale blond hair swinging. "It can't."

"It's okay, Miranda," Dex said. "I should probably get started on my homework, anyway."

"Okay," I said. I was a little disappointed that our conversation was ending so abruptly, but it was probably for the best. I knew Dex was worried about his schoolwork. Besides, Hannah was clearly not going to leave until I saw what Finn had done to the Web site.

"Have a good day tomorrow," Dex said.

"You, too. Bye," I said.

"Bye," he said.

"Bye, Dex," Hannah said.

As soon as the call ended, I typed in the URL for Hannah's Web site. Then I sat back, staring in openmouthed horror. The screen turned a fluorescent pink, so bright it hurt my eyeballs to look at it. MATCH MADE scrolled across the top in a hideous curly font. A cartoon cupid flew across the screen in the opposite direction, shooting arrows up into the name, which stuck into the *M*s. I was so distracted by this garish display that it took me a few moments before I was able to focus on the text:

Hey, Orange Cove High students. Are you a loser at love?
Are you too unattractive to find a date on your own?
Do people laugh hysterically when you ask them out?
Have no fear—help is on the way! Hannah Moore is here
to help you find romance.

Underneath, there was a picture of a beaming Hannah, with the words CALL ME blinking over her head. And then, under Hannah's picture:

Results guaranteed. If you're not entirely satisfied with your new romantic life, we'll double your money back.

"I hate to say I told you so, but . . . no, wait, I take it back. I don't hate saying it at all. I told you so. I told you not to trust Finn with this," I said.

"'Too unattractive to find a date' . . . 'Double your money back' . . . the stupid cupid," Hannah said. "It's just *horrible*. So, so horrible. Why would Finn do this to me? I was nice to him, wasn't I? I offered to pay him for doing the work!"

"Finn doesn't really need the money. He's made millions developing computer games," I said.

"Even so! Why would he want to ruin me?" Hannah bleated.

"First of all, this"—I gestured toward the computer screen—"does not ruin you. And second, this is how Finn amuses himself."

"Then why are you friends with him?"

I considered this. "I don't know. I never really thought about it. He is pretty funny."

"This is not funny," Hannah said.

It actually was a little funny, but I knew Hannah was not in the best state of mind to see the humor in it.

"We'll just take it down. I doubt anyone has seen it yet," I said.

"You think?" Hannah asked doubtfully.

"Didn't Finn say he just launched the Web site today? We're probably the only ones who've seen it." *Along with everyone he's told*, I thought, but didn't say out loud. Instead, I said, "We'll just take it offline, and it will be like it never happened."

This turned out to be easier said than done. Much easier. In fact, an hour later, Hannah and I were still trying to figure out how to disable the Web site. Finn had changed all of the passwords on Hannah's Web site software. Hannah tried calling Finn, but he—probably sensing her wrath—didn't pick up.

"I'm sorry. I just don't know enough about computers to fix this," I said. "Why don't you try contacting a computer repair shop? Maybe they have programmers on staff."

"No, I'll just find some computer geek at school and get him to do it for me," Hannah said moodily.

"How?"

She shrugged. "You know. I'll just talk to him. Smile at him. That's pretty much all it takes."

"And that worked out so well for you the last time," I said dryly. When Hannah looked confused, I clarified. "Wasn't Finn the last computer geek you tried charming into doing your work for you?"

"That's true. Maybe I should just hire a professional Web designer," Hannah said.

"Wise decision," I agreed.

Chapter Thirteen

The following Monday morning, I ran into Charlie in the school parking lot. She pulled into the space next to mine, just as I was climbing out of Bumblebee. Charlie was driving her family's ancient station wagon, which had once belonged to her mom before it had been passed down, in turn, to each of Charlie's older sisters, and finally to Charlie.

"Hey, Miranda," Charlie said, pulling her backpack out of the car and slamming the car door shut. "I feel like I haven't seen you in forever."

"That's because you haven't seen me in forever," I said. "I can't remember the last time we've had a conversation outside of class."

"I know. I'm sorry," Charlie said. "I've been a bad friend lately, haven't I?"

"No, it's okay. I know you've been busy painting," I said. We turned and walked toward school together.

"Yeah, but even so, I didn't mean to blow you off," Charlie said. "Especially since I know you've been bummed out ever since Dex left. What are you doing after school today?"

"Actually, nothing," I said. "My article for *The Ampersand* is due tomorrow, but I wrote it over the weekend. The only thing I have left to do is check it over for typos."

I was pleased with how my profile on Dex had turned out. He'd given me a lot of great quotes during our interview. I thought I'd succeeded in showing how conflicted he was over going away to school, while also highlighting his excitement at the opportunity to play for a top high school lacrosse team. I'd e-mailed the piece to Dex after I finished it to make sure he approved and that there wasn't anything in it that would embarrass him. He'd given it a big thumbs-up.

"Good for you," Charlie said.

"So do you want to do something?" I asked, perking up at the idea.

"Sure. Do you want to go to Grounded?" Charlie asked.

"Sounds great. You don't have to paint?"

"No, I can take an afternoon off. We need to catch up," Charlie said, bumping me with one shoulder. "Only don't tell Finn, okay?"

"Why not?" I asked, surprised.

"Because he'll insist on coming, too. And he'll spend the entire time cracking wise. Or, even worse, talking about his dimbo girlfriend," Charlie said darkly.

I had the definite feeling that Charlie hadn't fully exorcised her feelings for Finn through her unrequited-love-inspired paintings.

"Is *dimbo* even a word?"

"I don't know. If it's not, it should be. *Dumb* plus *bimbo* equals *dimbo*," Charlie said.

I thought this was a bit unfair. Phoebe was indisputably an airhead, but she really wasn't a bimbo. But I knew this wasn't a line of argument that Charlie would be open to.

"Gotcha. After school, at Grounded, no Finn," I said. "I'll just have to let Nora know I can't give her a ride home from school today."

"You can bring her along if you want," Charlie offered.

I considered this, but shook my head. I liked Nora and had enjoyed the time we'd been spending together, but, even so, I really wanted to spend some time alone with Charlie, so we could catch up.

"No, that's okay. Let's just keep it to the two of us. We haven't hung out on our own in ages," I said.

"Cool beans," Charlie said.

•

But that afternoon, moments after Charlie and I had settled in at our favorite table at Grounded, coffees in hand, the bell that hung on the glass front door of the coffee shop tinkled. I glanced up and saw Nora coming in. When she spotted us, she smiled and headed over to our table.

"Hey," Nora said. "I saw your car parked out in front, so I thought I'd come in and find you." She looked uncertainly from me to Charlie. "Unless I'm interrupting?"

I couldn't help thinking, *Yeah, you sort of are*, but I didn't want to hurt Nora's feelings. After all, she had no idea that Charlie and I had planned on having a catch-up session. I hadn't gone into detail when I told her I couldn't give her a ride home after school.

I shook my head and smiled. "Not at all."

"Take a seat," Charlie said.

"Great! I'll just go grab a coffee first," Nora said.

While she was at the counter, ordering her drink, I turned to Charlie. "Do you mind if she hangs out with us?" I asked, taking care to keep my voice low.

"No, it's fine," Charlie said, shaking her head. "She seems nice."

"She is," I said.

"Besides, it's not like we could tell her to go away, like we could with Finn," Charlie said with a grin. "I once told him that he was the poster boy for jerks everywhere, and he actually thought I was complimenting him."

"Who?" Nora asked, returning to the table with her latte just in time to hear Charlie's last words.

"Who else? Finn," Charlie said.

Nora sat down and blew on her coffee before taking a sip. "He's so funny."

Charlie shot her a dark look. "He certainly thinks he is."

Nora looked startled at the venom in Charlie's tone. I could tell she was worried she'd said something wrong.

"Don't worry," I told her. "Charlie and Finn have a love-hate relationship."

"Miranda!" Charlie said.

"Okay. They have a hate-hate relationship," I said, biting my lip in order to keep from smiling. I shot Nora a look, remembering that she'd guessed the real nature of Charlie's feelings for Finn. "Did I tell you guys what Finn did to Hannah's Web site?"

Nora had already heard the details of Finn's sabotage, but as Charlie hadn't, I filled her in.

"What an idiot," Charlie said, clearly referring to Finn and not Hannah. "What did Finn have to say about it?"

"He just laughed about it. He thought it was hilarious," I said.

"Has she fixed it?"

"Not yet. Finn changed all of the passwords on her Web site–hosting software, and now claims that he can't remember what he changed them to, so she can't get access to the account," I said.

"Hannah's furious. She said she's going to blackball Finn from all Orange Cove High functions."

"Does Finn know that?" Nora asked, looking concerned.

"Like he'd care," Charlie said, rolling her eyes. "Although maybe it'll finally motivate him to start studying, so he doesn't fail out of Geek High and end up at Orange Cove High."

"Doubtful," I said.

"Seriously. This is Finn we're talking about," Charlie agreed.

"I have a friend like Finn back in Boston," Nora said. "He jokes around constantly. And he's really funny, but sometimes it can be irritating. You know, if you're trying to have a serious conversation about something."

"Exactly," Charlie said, pointing a finger in Nora's direction. "That's it exactly. I know Finn can be funny, but sometimes you want to discuss something other than what superpowers would be passed on if Spider-Man and Wonder Woman had a baby together."

"Especially since Spider-Man and Wonder Woman aren't even from the same comic book series," I said. I knew this only because I'd been present at the discussion, during which Finn—after lengthy deliberation—decided that for the purposes of a hypothetical question, it was okay that the two superheroes came from different fictional worlds. Charlie had finally threatened to stick chewed gum into his laptop if he didn't shut up about it.

Charlie shot me a death-ray look. Nora caught it, and hurried to change the subject.

"So, Charlie, Miranda tells me that you're a really amazing artist," Nora said.

"You said that I'm amazing?" Charlie asked me, her expression instantly softening.

I nodded. "Because it's true. You should see her work sometime, Nora. Charlie has an art studio in her house."

"I'd love to," Nora said.

"Do you like art?" Charlie asked.

"Absolutely," Nora said enthusiastically. "I used to go to the Museum of Fine Arts in Boston all the time."

Nora's answer took me by complete surprise. She'd never mentioned to me that she was interested in art.

Is she just pretending to be interested so Charlie will like her? I wondered. Maybe. But it didn't really matter. Didn't everyone feign interest in things they weren't really into from time to time? I knew Nora was shy and still trying to fit in at Geek High. It wasn't surprising that she'd make an extra effort to get along with Charlie or Finn.

But the thing was, I wasn't all that interested in art. And Charlie knew that. So I couldn't even pretend to be interested, as Nora asked Charlie about the local museums, and Charlie enthusiastically told her about a show she'd been to over the summer at the Norton Museum of Art in downtown West Palm Beach. Instead, I drank my coffee and people watched as students from both Geek High and Orange Cove High trailed in and out of Grounded, and tried to focus on how it was a good thing that Nora and Charlie were getting along so well. After four years of listening to Charlie and Finn bicker about everything from the free market to which was the best flavor of SpaghettiOs, I knew all too well how hard life could be when your friends didn't get along.

*

After we'd been at Grounded for about an hour, and I was reaching my limit on how much longer I could listen to Charlie enthuse about Picasso's Blue Period, the bell on Grounded's front door jingled. I looked up in time to see a very glum-looking Finn arrive.

"Oh, no," Charlie groaned, catching sight of Finn at the same time I did.

But I was glad to see Finn, if for no other reason than to break up the monotony of the art talk.

"Hey," I called out to him. "Over here."

"Miranda," Charlie hissed.

"What? Like he's not going to see us sitting here?" I said.

Nora craned her head around to see who we were talking about. "Finn looks sad," she commented.

She was right. Finn did look sad. His shoulders were slumped and his hands were stuffed into his pockets. Even his Mohawk was drooping.

"Hi," he said dully, as he collapsed into the empty chair at our table.

"Are you okay?" I asked.

Finn shrugged. "I guess," he said.

Charlie and I exchanged a look. A Finn who didn't bounce around like Tigger jacked up on caffeine, while wisecracking non-stop, was a Finn to be concerned about.

"Did something happen?" Charlie asked in a much nicer tone than she normally used with Finn.

Finn shrugged again, but then he heaved out a great sigh and said, "Phoebe broke up with me."

I stole another look at Charlie to see how she was absorbing this information, but this time, she didn't meet my eyes.

"I'm sorry, Finn," I said sympathetically.

"Yeah, that's too bad," Charlie said, somehow managing to sound like she meant it.

"Did she tell you why?" Nora asked.

Our combined sympathy seemed to have a positive effect on Finn. He perked up a bit, straightening his shoulders and leaning back in his chair. He stretched his long legs out in front of him—which meant Charlie had to move to make room for him—but amazingly, she did so without yelling at him.

"She claims it's because I spend too much time playing video games. But that can't be it, can it? I think your stepsister might have had something to do with it, Miranda," Finn said.

"Hannah? Why?" I asked.

"I don't know for sure. It's just a feeling I have. Maybe Hannah told Phoebe that if she didn't dump me, she'd spread a rumor about her around school. Girls are evil that way," Finn said darkly.

"Not *all* girls," Charlie said.

I shook my head. "No way. Hannah wouldn't do that."

"How can you be so sure? She was pretty nasty to me on the phone the other day," Finn said. "She said I have no moral center. Can you believe that? Me! I mean, I almost only play Neutral-Good aligned Dungeons & Dragons characters." Finn tapped his fingers together. "Well, unless I'm playing a wizard above the tenth level. But that only makes sense. What's the point of being good if you're wielding that much power?"

Ignoring his Dungeons & Dragons tangent, I decided to point out the obvious. "Hannah's mad at you because you screwed up her Web site. But I know Hannah. She wouldn't have threatened to spread a mean rumor about Phoebe just to get back at you."

At least, I hope she wouldn't, I thought, remembering just how angry Hannah had been at Finn.

"Maybe I should get Hannah to set me up with one of her hottie friends," Finn mused.

Charlie flinched, but Finn didn't notice.

I stared at him. "Please tell me you're not serious," I said.

"Why wouldn't I be?" I asked.

"Did you forget the entire conversation we just had two seconds ago about Hannah being so mad at you, you think she'd sabotage your relationship with Phoebe?" I asked.

"I see your point," Finn said. "But if Hannah's really the professional matchmaker she claims to be, she shouldn't let that stand in her way of setting me up."

"Didn't you and Phoebe just break up, like, five minutes ago?" Charlie said. She crossed her arms and looked at Finn with a bit more than her usual severity.

"So?" Finn asked.

"You need to mourn the relationship," Nora suggested. "Take some time to reflect on what went wrong, so you don't repeat the same mistakes in the future."

"Nah," Finn said. "I just need a new honey. That's the best cure. And it would be the perfect revenge on Phoebe for dumping me, so, you know, bonus."

I glanced at my watch. "I should get going. My article is due tomorrow, and I want to reread it before I hand it in." I glanced at Nora. "Do you want a ride home?"

"Or I can drop you off, if you want to stay a little longer," Charlie suggested. "You said you wanted to hear more about the Rothko exhibit."

"Oh, yawn," Finn said. "Can't we talk about something that doesn't make me want to pass out with boredom?"

"You don't have to stay if you don't want to hear about it," Charlie said.

"Nah, that's okay. I'll stick around so I can mock you," Finn said.

"Bye, everyone," I said.

On my way out, I glanced back at the table. Nora, Charlie, and Finn were all in animated conversation. And even though it had been my choice to leave, and even though I really did want to reread my article, I couldn't help feeling a little left out.

Chapter Fourteen

When I arrived back at the beach house, Avery's car was parked in the driveway. My heart sank. Avery was the last person I wanted to see right now.

As I shut the front door behind me, I could hear voices in the kitchen.

"Hi, I'm home," I called out.

Willow appeared, wriggling with happiness. She stuck her long nose in my hand in greeting, and I patted her head.

"Hi, girl," I said. I bent down to give her a hug.

Willow followed me as I headed toward the kitchen. As much as I'd like to avoid Avery, I was hungry and wanted a snack. Besides, the beach house was my home now. *I have every right to be here*, I reminded myself. I wasn't going to skulk off to my room to hide from Avery. So what if she was mean? Sticks and stones, and all of that.

But the scene in the kitchen startled me so much, all thoughts of Avery's hostilities disappeared.

For one thing, Avery and Hannah weren't alone. There was a boy there with them. And he wasn't at all the sort of guy they normally hung out with. He was very short and very thin, and had unfortunately bushy hair and long sideburns. He couldn't have been older than fourteen.

He has to be a freshman, I thought. And I doubted Hannah had hung out with geeky freshman guys even when she was a freshman herself.

To make the situation even odder, the boy was perched on a stool in front of a white sheet that had been hung from the upper kitchen cupboards, creating a solid drape behind him. Avery had a camcorder set up on a tripod and pointed at him, and appeared to be filming him. Hannah stood to one side, a clipboard in hand and a Bluetooth in her ear. The boy looked absolutely miserable.

"What do you think your best features are?" Avery barked at the boy, who cringed and glanced around as though looking for an escape route.

"I'm not sure," he finally said. "Maybe my hair?"

"I meant personality-wise. We're going to do a complete make-over on you to solve your physical shortcomings. At least, to the best of our ability. We can't do anything about your height," Avery said. Then, as though realizing that this might be just a tad harsh, she added, "Don't worry. Maybe you'll have a growth spurt soon. Your dad's not freakishly short, is he?"

"He's pretty short," the boy said miserably.

"Too bad," Avery said. "Hannah, make a note about that. Likely to stay short."

"Got it," Hannah said, scribbling on her clipboard.

"What's going on?" I asked.

"Hey, Miranda," Hannah said. "Meet Match Made's first official client—Leo Trachtenberg."

"Wait. I'm your first client?" Leo asked worriedly. "You didn't tell me that. I thought you had experience with this."

"I do. I've set up tons of people," Hannah assured him. "In fact,

Miranda here is one of my success stories. I got her together with her boyfriend."

"Why are you filming him?" I asked.

"Actually, you're the one who gave me the idea," Hannah said.

"I did?" I asked, confused.

"Don't you remember? It was when you asked me if we were going to put up pictures of our clients on the Web site?" Hannah said.

"Yeah, but I thought you said"—I was about to repeat what Hannah had said, that she wasn't running a dating service for the sort of losers who would post their pictures on a dating Web site, but then, glancing at Leo, decided to change tactics—"you didn't want to do that."

"That was before, when I was going to cater my matchmaking services to, ah"—this time Hannah looked at Leo, as though she, too, was worried about saying something in front of him that might hurt his feelings—"more discriminating clients," she finished delicately.

"What she means is that the entire Orange Cove High School already knows I'm a loser who can't get a date, so I don't have a lot to lose," Leo translated for me.

"You have to stop talking about yourself that way," Hannah chided him. "Remember, the image you portray to the outside world is very important. If you start truly believing that you're an attractive, successful, likeable guy, other people will start seeing you that way."

Leo rolled his eyes. "Believing that I'm Brad Pitt isn't going to magically turn me into Brad Pitt."

"Maybe not. But you don't have to be Brad Pitt to find love," Hannah told him.

Hannah was actually making sense to me. I wondered if I should be worried.

"Were you finally able to fix your Web site?" I asked Hannah.

"No. But it actually turned out to be a good thing. People thought it was really funny, especially the part about being a *loser at love* and *too ugly to find a date*. Word got around, and we started to get some clients because of it," Hannah said.

"People want to hire a matchmaking service that calls them ugly losers?" I asked.

Hannah shrugged. "I guess people found the honesty refreshing. Anyway, we decided that since a lot of our clients are, um,"—she gave Leo another furtive glance—"appearance challenged, we'd expand our services to offer them makeovers. You know, counsel them on how to look better, dress better, feel better about themselves. After we're done with Leo's intake video, Avery and I are going to take him to get his hair cut."

"What? But I don't want to get my hair cut. I like my hair like this," Leo said. He covered his head with both hands, as though to ward off a surprise attack.

"You have to get it cut," Avery told him bossily. "No girl is going to want to date you with those sideburns. Total Loserville."

"So you're not mad at Finn anymore?" I asked Hannah.

Her eyes narrowed. "Oh, no. I'm still mad at him. In fact, one of these days I'll get him back for what he did."

There was something menacing in the way Hannah said this.

"You didn't happen to say anything to Phoebe about Finn, did you?" I asked. "Something that would make her break up with him?"

"No. Why?"

"Just wondering."

"Maybe I should, though," Hannah said thoughtfully. "Maybe I should tell her that you told me he's obsessed with feet. Or that he collects Madame Alexander Dolls. Which do you think would freak her out more?"

"Hannah!" I said.

"It's just a thought," she said.

"It's a bad thought. And don't drag me into your revenge plots," I said. "Besides, the reason I asked is that Finn and Phoebe broke up."

"They did? Really?" Hannah tapped a thoughtful fingernail against her clipboard. "So Finn's on the market? Maybe I could hook him up with one of my clients. Does he have a problem with severe overbites?"

Meanwhile, Avery and Leo were still arguing about his hair.

"But the sideburns are my signature look. And it took me forever to grow them out," Leo said, clearly not ready to give in on this point.

"So?" Avery said, clearly not moved. "You can always grow them out again. But trust me, you'll look so much better without those things. You can't go around with your head looking like a Chia Pet."

"If I'm going to find a girlfriend, shouldn't she like me for who I am and not what I look like?" Leo asked.

Avery gave him a patronizing smile. "If you could find a girl who liked you for who you are, you wouldn't need us. We're going to turn you into someone new. Someone better."

Leo looked so miserable, I decided I had to intervene on his behalf.

"Hannah, can I talk to you for a minute? Alone?" I asked.

Hannah glanced at her watch—clearly she didn't think there was any time to be wasted before she bullied Leo into getting a haircut—but finally she acquiesced.

"Okay," she said. "But make it quick."

Hannah and I headed out to the back deck, with Willow tagging along behind us. The deck was raised on stilts, and offered a gorgeous view of the Atlantic Ocean. Willow stuck her nose out between the railings and stared longingly at the sandpipers darting along at the water's edge.

As soon as the glass door was shut behind her, Hannah said, "What's up?"

"I don't think you should bully that poor kid into cutting off his sideburns if he doesn't want to," I said.

"Why not?"

"Because he's a person. With feelings. And it isn't cool to keep talking about him like he's some sort of a freakish loser," I said. "He seems like a perfectly nice kid."

"I don't think he's a freakish loser. That's how he sees himself," Hannah said.

"How do you know?"

"He came to us after seeing our Web site. Remember? *Are you a loser at love? Are you too unattractive to find a date?* If he didn't think those things about himself, he wouldn't have hired us," Hannah pointed out.

"It's one thing for him to have low self-esteem. It's another thing for you to make him feel even worse about himself," I argued.

"That's just it—we're trying to help him feel *better* about himself," Hannah said.

"By telling him he needs to have a makeover?" I asked.

"Yes. The problem with you, Miranda, is that you're too idealistic. You think people should always be judged on who they are, not what they look like," Hannah said.

"What's wrong with that?" I asked.

"It's not realistic. The truth is, looks do matter. And people do judge you on what you look like. Take you, for example," Hannah said.

"What about me?" I asked, instantly wary.

"Remember how you used to dress? All you used to wear were boring T-shirts and ratty old jeans. Then I took you shopping, and we got you some cute new clothes, and you look like an entirely different person," Hannah said.

"I don't know about the *entirely different* part," I said.

"Trust me, you do. And look at the effect it's having on your life. You told me that witchy girl you go to school with wanted to say something mean to you about your appearance, but couldn't come up with anything," Hannah said. "And look at your friend Nora."

"Nora? What about her?" I asked, startled.

"She's started dressing like you."

"She has?"

"Yes. Haven't you noticed? I noticed it the other day when she was over here. She totally copied that outfit you have. You know, the cute tunic with the spaghetti straps over the skinny-leg jeans. The top was exactly the same as yours, only she had it in green instead. I remember seeing it at the store, but I thought blue was a better color on you," Hannah said.

"No, I hadn't noticed," I said, completely bewildered. "But I have no fashion sense. Why would anyone copy what I wear?"

"That's what I'm telling you. You may not have any fashion sense, but you *look* like you do, thanks to me. So everyone who sees you thinks that you've got great style. And then they want to copy you. Or at least Nora does," Hannah said.

"But isn't it sort of weird that she'd copy me like that?" I asked. The idea made me vaguely uneasy.

"No. I mean, it might be sort of psycho if she bought all of the exact same clothes as you. But if she's just copying a piece or two, that's not so weird. You know what they say about imitation being the sincerest form of flattery," Hannah said.

Hannah's cell phone rang, and she tapped her Bluetooth on. "Match Made matchmaking, Hannah Moore speaking. Yes, that's right. Hold one minute, please." Hannah looked at me. "Are we done, Miranda? This is a client calling."

"Yeah, we're done," I said.

I hadn't succeeded in talking Hannah into leaving Leo's hair alone. But, after all, it was his head. If he didn't want his hair cut, he was going to have to stand firm.

But Hannah's comments about Nora wearing the same clothes as me worried me. The long tunic tank top wasn't the first item of clothing Nora had copied from me; she'd also bought an identical plaid halter top. And maybe there were other things she'd copied, as well, without my noticing. I never did pay much attention to what people were wearing. For all I knew, Nora *could* have bought all the exact same clothes I had. Which would be really creepy.

But no, I thought, and shook off this thought. Why was my mind jumping to such nasty places? If Nora and I had some of the same clothes, it was just a coincidence. Orange Cove was a small town, with a limited number of places to shop.

I thought I knew what was going on. I was still feeling a little jealous about how well Nora had been getting along with Charlie and Finn that afternoon. In fact, it wasn't the only time I'd been feeling flashes of jealousy lately. I'd also been jealous of Tabitha for getting the fiction assignment for *The Ampersand,* and I'd worried unnecessarily about Dex being invited to a study group, for no other reason than that the person who'd issued the invitation happened to be a girl.

I have to stop being so jealous, I told myself sternly, as I headed back inside the beach house. There was a reason they called jealousy the green-eyed monster. As soon as you let it loose, it started to rampage out of control, insidiously causing you to question everyone and everything around you.

"Come on, Willow," I called out. She was still at the deck fence, only now she'd wedged her entire head and neck through the railings to get a better look at the birds below. Willow panicked when she tried to turn to look back at me and realized that the fence post was in her way. When she finally freed herself, she looked sheepish as she trotted past me into the house.

In the kitchen, Leo was still on his stool, but the white sheet that had been tacked up behind him was now wrapped around his shoulders. Avery was standing over Leo, brandishing electric clippers in one hand while keeping a firm grip on Leo's chin with her free hand. She looked intently down at him, while turning his chin from side to side.

"What are you doing to him?" I asked.

Avery and Leo both looked up at me. And as soon as they did, I could see exactly what she'd been doing to him: in our absence, one of Leo's sideburns had been shaved off.

"I'm making him look better," Avery said.

I considered trying to help Leo—insisting that he had the right to wear his sideburns however he chose, and that she should let him go immediately. But then I remembered what Hannah had said about how I was too idealistic, and that maybe Leo really would be happier once the ridiculous sideburns were gone. Besides, he couldn't walk around with one sideburn short and the other long.

So I just said, "Oh."

Avery refocused her attention on Leo's hair. She picked up a pair of scissors and snipped them menacingly. "I think an inch or two overall would make a big difference," she said.

"An inch or *two*? But my hair's only about two and a half inches long!" Leo said nervously. "Can't I at least go to a professional barber?"

"Why? I can totally do this. Besides, if you're ever going to have a relationship, you're going to need to work on your trust issues," Avery said.

Recognizing a lost cause, I grabbed an apple and headed off to my room to give my *Ampersand* piece one final read through.

Chapter Fifteen

Dex was in brighter spirits that night. He'd gotten a B-plus on his first homework assignment in European history.

"Now if I could just figure out my trig homework, I'd be golden," Dex said.

"Too bad you don't know anyone who's good at math. Especially a girlfriend willing to help you out," I said.

"I didn't even think of that. Can you help me?"

"Sure. Just give me the problems, and we'll go through each one step-by-step," I suggested.

"Have I ever told you that you're the best girlfriend ever?" Dex asked.

"Yes. But I'm always open to hearing it again," I said.

The truth was, I was glad to have the distraction. I'd been feeling off all afternoon, ever since leaving Grounded. But an hour spent walking Dex through the complexities of trigonometry had the effect of clearing my mind. After we hung up—and I was pleased by how reluctant Dex seemed to say good-bye to me—Charlie called me on my cell phone.

"Hey. I wanted to make sure you were okay," she said. "You were so quiet this afternoon. You didn't seem like your usual self."

"What do you mean?" I asked. I'd been sitting at my desk while I Skyped with Dex, but now I moved over to my bed, sitting cross-legged on top of the blue-and-green bedspread. Willow stood, tail wagging, and mashed her head down on the edge of the bed so I could stroke her nose.

"I feel like I spent the whole time we were at Grounded talking to Nora," Charlie said.

You did spend the whole time talking to Nora. I was completely superfluous to the conversation, I wanted to say. But then, remembering my resolution to squelch such jealous thoughts, I instead said, "I guess I was just off in my own little world."

"Anything you want to talk about?" Charlie offered.

"No, nothing like that. I think I'm just nervous about my article for *The Ampersand*. I'm handing it in tomorrow," I said. This wasn't a complete lie. I thought I'd done a good job with it, but I was nervous about how Candace would respond. I had the feeling that she read all of *The Ampersand* pieces with a very critical eye.

"Are you happy with how it came out?" Charlie asked.

"I think so," I said. "Or, at least, I hope so. I just don't want Candace to hate it."

"I'm sure she'll love it," Charlie said supportively.

"Let's talk about something else," I suggested. "This is just making me nervous."

"Okay. Like what?"

"We could talk about Finn's big news," I said.

"What do you mean?" Charlie asked.

"Stop playing innocent. You know exactly what I'm talking about," I said.

"I can't say I'm surprised he and Phoebe broke up," Charlie said. "They had nothing in common."

"It just seems like it went downhill quickly. When we saw them at

Grounded together that time, Phoebe seemed like she was really into Finn," I said.

Charlie hesitated. "Do you think Finn meant it about getting Hannah to set him up with another girl?"

"Yes," I said. "But I wouldn't worry too much. Hannah's decided to work with more, um, how shall I put it? Challenging clients."

"How so?"

"When she heard Finn was newly single, she asked me if he'd have a problem dating someone with a severe overbite," I said. "Besides, Hannah's still annoyed with Finn for messing with her Web site."

"That's good," Charlie said, sounding more cheerful.

"You know what I'm going to say now, right?" I asked.

Charlie sighed heavily. "You're not going to start lecturing me about how I should talk to Finn and tell him how I feel about him, are you?" she asked.

"That's right," I said, choosing to ignore the lecture crack. I never lectured her. I just offered advice. Succinct, to-the-point, very useful advice.

"What's the point?" Charlie said. "We've been over this a million times. I can't just walk up to Finn and say, 'Look, you may be a complete freak, but I'm in love with you.'"

"I'd leave out the freak part. But that's just me," I said.

"I can't do it. I just can't," Charlie said.

"Why not?"

"Because I'm a chicken. I admit it. I'm a total coward," Charlie said.

"You? No way. You're one of the bravest people I know," I said.

Charlie snorted. "Please," she said.

"I'm serious. Look at your artwork. You put all of your emotions and hopes and dreams into your paintings. That's really brave. I can't even write one measly little article without worrying that it's going to be criticized. You've had, what, a dozen art shows?" I said.

Charlie was quiet for a moment. "But that's not nearly as scary as telling Finn how I feel about him."

"I don't think it really is that different," I said.

"Maybe I should talk to Hannah about this. She's the professional, right? Maybe she'll have some matchmaking advice for me," Charlie said.

I sighed and leaned back on a fluffy stack of pillows. Willow, realizing her head stroking had come to an end, returned to her circular bed with a snuffling sigh. "You know what I think?"

"What?"

"I think you have to stop listening to me or to Hannah or anyone else. In the end, you have to do what *you* think is right. What you want to do. It's your life, after all," I said. "You're the one who has to live it."

"Maybe you're right," Charlie said.

"It's bound to happen once or twice in my life," I said.

Charlie laughed. "More often than that, I think. By the way, what are you doing Saturday?"

"We're driving down to the Keys for the weekend," I said.

"Really? I didn't know that," Charlie said.

"I've hardly seen you," I reminded her. "But while we're on the subject, I've been meaning to ask you: Will you watch Willow while we're away?"

"No problem," Charlie said.

"Do you want to check with your mom first?" I asked. Mrs. Teague was allergic to most animals, and dogs in particular gave her sneezing fits.

"Nah, she won't mind, as long as I keep Willow in my room," Charlie said. "Are you missing school?"

"We're leaving Friday morning, so I'll miss that day. Orange Cove High has the day off. I think Hannah said it's a teacher workday, or something," I said. It was typical of Peyton to schedule this family getaway around Hannah's schedule, and expect me just to go along with it. I hated missing school. It always meant extra catch-up work when you returned. "Why, what are you doing?"

"Nora and I were talking about heading down to West Palm to see the Georgia O'Keeffe show at the Norton," Charlie said. "And she's never been to Palm Beach, so we were going to go walk around there after. I was going to see if you wanted to go with us."

And just like that, the green-eyed monster reared up again. Nora and Charlie made plans without me? Even if Charlie had decided to include me, it was after the fact. Would Nora and Charlie get even closer this weekend? And if so, what did that mean for me? Would I be replaced? Would I—

But then I stopped myself.

It's totally fine for Charlie and Nora to hang out together, I reminded myself. I was not going to get all twisted up with jealousy. I took a deep breath and tried to will the green-eyed monster away. It didn't work right away, so I took a few more deep breaths until I started to feel calm.

"Miranda? Are you there?" Charlie asked.

"Yes, I'm here," I said.

"Why aren't you saying anything?"

"Oh, I just . . . got distracted for a minute. Willow was making a funny sound," I lied.

Willow, hearing her name, opened one amber eye and thumped her tail.

"Is she okay?"

"Um, yeah, she's fine," I said.

"I'm really glad you met Nora. She seems really cool. It's nice to talk to someone who's into art," Charlie said.

"I actually didn't know she was into art," I said. "That was news to me."

"Really? Well, anyway, she seemed really interested in listening to me talk about it," Charlie said. "I hope I wasn't boring her."

"I'm sure you weren't," I said.

Charlie and I chatted for a few more minutes, and then she got off the phone, saying she wanted to get some painting done before bedtime. But for a long time after we hung up, I stayed put, lying on my bed and staring up at the bumpy white ceiling, thinking about Nora. She talked to Charlie about art, joked around with Finn, and with me . . . with me, she talked about her long-distance boyfriend. Was that all genuine Nora? Or was it just a chameleon attempt to fit in with us? And, if so, would I ever get to know which was the real Nora?

Chapter Sixteen

"I can't wait to get to the resort," Hannah said. "I'm going to lie out by the pool and work on my tan."

Hannah had spent most of the car ride down to the Keys plugged into her iPod, but as we drove down the Overseas Highway, with its sweeping views of the Atlantic Ocean, she abandoned her music in favor of planning her vacation weekend, the extent of which seemed to be sunning herself and painting her nails. I'd spent the long drive working on a short story about a teenage girl aspiring to be a matchmaker, which was inspired by Hannah.

Dad and Peyton exchanged a significant look from the front seat. That should have been my first clue that something was up.

"I thought you didn't believe in tanning, because it gives you wrinkles," I said.

"I think that's only if you get really, really dark. Or burned. If you just get a nice golden shade, it isn't that bad for you," Hannah said.

"I thought I read somewhere that any prolonged sun exposure is bad for your skin," I said.

"Really? Well, maybe by the time I get old, scientists will have found a cure for wrinkles," Hannah said. "In fact, maybe Emmett will be the one to discover it. Wouldn't that be cool? I should tell him to develop a wrinkle cream for the science fair instead of a solar-powered car."

"I think attempting to discover how to reverse human aging might be a little too large of a topic for him to tackle in time for the science fair," I pointed out.

"Why? Emmett's really good at science. He might as well put his talent to use," Hannah said. "So, what are you planning to do this weekend, Miranda? You don't play tennis, do you?"

"No. I played once and I got hit in the face with a ball. So that was pretty much the end of my tennis career. What else is there to do at the resort?" I asked.

"I'm not sure. But these places usually have tennis courts and a golf course and a spa. Hey, that's what we'll do. We'll go get some spa treatments together," Hannah said. "Mom, do you want to do that with Miranda and me?"

Peyton didn't answer. Instead, she and my dad exchanged another significant look.

"What's going on?" I asked, instantly suspicious. Something was definitely up.

Dad cleared his throat. "Girls, we have something to tell you."

"What?" Hannah said.

Dad took a deep breath and glanced again at Peyton. She was hiding behind enormous sunglasses, and didn't seem too eager to jump in and help him out.

"We didn't exactly tell you the whole truth about what we're doing this weekend," Dad said slowly. This sounded so ominous, I half expected to hear menacing music kick up in the background. Dum dum *dum*.

"But you haven't told us anything," I said. "Just that we're going to a resort in the Keys for the weekend. Which part of that wasn't true?"

"The resort part," Dad said.

Hannah and I looked at each other in alarm.

"So, what? We're staying at a hotel, or a bed and breakfast instead?" Hannah asked hopefully.

"No, it's more of a . . ." Dad's voice trailed off, and he waved one hand in the air, as though that clarified anything.

"A *what*, Dad?" I asked.

"A campground," Dad finished.

This time, Hannah and I stared at each other in horror.

I don't camp. My dad had taken me camping once before—right after he and my mom split up, and he was going through a phase where he kept wanting to spend quality time with me—and it was a total disaster. It was hot and buggy, and on our first night there, raccoons got into the food and ate or carried off everything we'd brought with us. On the second night, it started to pour, and we learned the hard way that our borrowed tent had several big holes in it.

After that disastrous trip, I swore I'd never go camping again. And I was fairly sure Hannah felt the same way. She thought she was roughing it if she had to stay at a hotel with fewer than four stars.

"This is a joke, right?" Hannah asked hopefully. "A really, really lame joke?"

"No joke," Dad said.

"Mom?" Hannah asked.

"It was Dr. Patel's idea," Peyton said, referring to the marriage therapist she and Dad began seeing over the summer.

"It's a retreat," Dad chimed in. "They have all sorts of activities planned that are designed to bring us closer together as a family. And we'll sleep in tents and roast marshmallows over the campfire. Old-fashioned family fun. Just wait; it'll be great."

This was getting worse and worse. Hannah looked at me, shaking her head in disbelief.

"Why would we go camping when there are perfectly nice luxury hotels to stay in?" Hannah asked.

"Yeah, I'm going to have to agree with Hannah here," I said. "I have homework to do. I need to stay somewhere where I can plug in my laptop."

"No homework this weekend," Dad said. "We're going to focus all of our energy on making our family stronger."

"You aren't seriously going to make us do this, are you, Mom?" Hannah asked.

I thought Hannah was wise to appeal to her mother. I couldn't picture Peyton sleeping in a tent or building a campfire. She had perfectly sculpted nails, hair that was blown out three times a week by her stylist, and wore immaculate clothes in shades of white and ice blue. In fact, watching Peyton cope with the great outdoors might be the only bright spot of the weekend. The Ice Queen versus Mother Nature.

"We'll just have to make the best of it," Peyton said, sounding unhappily resigned.

"That's the spirit," Dad said cheerfully. "We're going to have such a good time this weekend, you'll be begging to go camping again."

"That," Hannah said darkly, "is never going to happen."

◆

Happy Camper Campground was located on Big Pine Key next to a small, murky lake. Dad parked the SUV on a dirt parking lot, and we checked in with the camp coordinator in the main building, which was basically a cinderblock shack with a few oscillating fans that swirled the hot air around. We made our way past the outdoor seating area—a ring of logs circling a flagpole, at the top of which the American flag waved limply—and headed toward the tents, which were, thankfully, already set up in six rows. We were assigned to two tents at the end of the second row. Hannah and I were sharing one tent; Dad and Peyton shared the other.

When we reached our tent, I peeked inside. Inside, there were two cots with foam mattresses.

"At least we won't have to sleep on the ground," I said.

"I wonder how many people are going to be here," Hannah said, looking at the other tents. A few families had already arrived and were starting to unload their cars. "Do you think all of these tents are reserved?"

"No idea," I said. "But these tents are pitched so close together, we'll be able to hear if anyone snores."

"This just gets worse and worse," Hannah muttered.

We made a few trips back and forth between the SUV and the tents, bringing our luggage and a big blue cooler, which, thankfully, contained food. I'd been half afraid that Dad was going to announce we'd have to fish for our dinner. An unpleasant moment arrived when we discovered that although my dad had stashed four sleeping bags in the back of the car—hidden behind the suitcases—he'd forgotten to pack pillows.

"How are we supposed to sleep without pillows?" Hannah asked. She had wheeled her enormous hot pink suitcase over the bumpy dirt path. The suitcase hadn't weathered the short trip well. It was now covered with dust, and grass was stuck in the wheels.

"You can fold up a sweatshirt and use that as a pillow," Dad said.

"Please tell me you're kidding," Hannah said grumpily.

"Maybe we could go into town and find a store that sells pillows," Peyton suggested.

"That's a great idea. And while we're there, we can check into a hotel," I said.

"Come on, girls. You have to adjust your attitudes," Dad said.

"We're not here to go shopping. We're here to rough it. The early pioneers didn't have pillows when they crossed the country in covered wagons, did they? We can survive without some creature comforts for a few days."

"Wait," I said as something occurred to me. "Where are the toilets?"

"I'm not sure," Dad said, looking around.

A scruffy-looking twenty-something guy wearing an I'M A HAPPY CAMPER T-shirt was passing by with a portable hibachi.

"Excuse me. Where are the bathrooms?" Dad asked him.

"The latrines are located on the other end of the camp," the camp counselor replied.

"Thanks," Dad said.

"Latrines?" I said. "Did he just say *latrines*?"

"I guess there isn't any indoor plumbing. We really are going to be roughing it this weekend," Dad said happily.

By now, Peyton was looking as horrified as Hannah and me.

"But there are showers, right? *Please* tell me there are showers," Peyton said.

"You don't need a shower," Dad said. "Just jump into the lake with a bar of soap."

"Do we know for sure that there aren't any alligators in that lake?" I asked.

Peyton's horror turned to alarm. "For God's sake, Richard. We're not bathing in alligator-infested water."

A whistle blew. The other families began to stir—standing, stretching, crawling out of the tent flaps—and turned to head toward the flagpole.

"What does the whistle mean?" Peyton asked.

"I think we're supposed to meet the program director," Dad said. "We should go see what's going on."

•

Twenty minutes later, Dad, Peyton, Hannah, and I were sitting un-
comfortably on the ring of logs, surrounded by a dozen other families. There was a lot of variation in the ages of our fellow campers.
Some of the family groups consisted of all adults—parents in their
sixties or older, accompanied by adult children. Others had kids
younger than Hannah and me. Oddly, everyone—everyone but
Hannah, Peyton, and me, that was—seemed really excited about
being there. I wondered whether they'd all found out about the complete lack of indoor plumbing yet.

Our group leader stood in front of us, beaming.

"Welcome to our Family Togetherness Weekend at Happy
Camper Campground," he said. "I'm the head happy camper, Chaz
Lundgren. Feel free to call me Chaz."

He didn't look like a Chaz to me. He wasn't slick with gelled-
back hair and a tight black T-shirt. Instead, he was short and stooped,
with thinning gray hair that he wore back in a stringy ponytail. He
wore a lime green I'M A HAPPY CAMPER T-shirt tucked into pleated
jeans.

"We've been running these Family Togetherness retreats for over
ten years. And I think the program just keeps getting stronger. Families
come from all over Florida to attend our retreats. Our goal this weekend is to bring you closer together as a family. We have a series of activities planned that will hopefully challenge you to work together,
rely on one another, and, ultimately, learn to trust one another more,"
Chaz continued.

Chaz had an odd, lilting way of talking, as though he were sure
that he was being incredibly persuasive. The effect of this was undermined by a slight lisp and a tendency to emphasize every fourth word,

regardless of whether it made sense in the context of what he was saying.

Hannah and I exchanged dark looks. Camping was bad enough. Being forced to participate in a series of planned group activities was an extra layer of awful.

"I'm going to divide you into groups," Chaz continued. "Group One will participate in a series of trust-strengthening exercises, such as Feeling Charades and role-playing exercises. Group Two will cook a meal together. And Group Three will be the first to attempt the rope course!"

Peyton murmured, "Rope course? I don't think so!"

But my Dad gave her a quelling look, and Peyton fell silent. She still looked mutinous, though.

*

As luck would have it, we were assigned Group Three.

The rope course turned out to be an obstacle course, consisting of a long series of rope ladders, rope swings, and large wooden structures we had to climb over. Everyone had to wear helmets, and our individual scores were tallied in one family score. Considering that I was allergic to any activity that made me sweat, and Peyton and Hannah were loathe to engage in anything that might result in a broken nail, I didn't rate our chances of winning as very good. Dad was enthusiastic, but he wasn't particularly athletic. Worse, the course—as explained by Chaz, who had accompanied us out there, along with his bullhorn—was set up so that we were forced to help one another out. For example, the first team member who made it over a climbing structure was supposed to assist his or her team members over. Likewise, the rope swing was nearly impossible to maneuver on your own; you needed a team member to hold it steady for you while you climbed on.

"You have got to be kidding me," Hannah said, standing with her arms crossed over her bebe tank top. "There's no way we're going to be able to do this."

"Not with that sort of attitude," Dad said. "There's no *me* in *team*."

His optimism was really starting to annoy me. And, from the expressions on Peyton's and Hannah's faces, Dad was having the same effect on them.

"What does that even mean?" Hannah said. "There's no *me* in *team*? That doesn't make any sense."

"And it's not even true. If you take away the *t* and the *a*, and switch around the *m* and the *e*, you do have *me*," I said.

"Richard, I *really* don't want to do this," Peyton said. She adjusted her helmet, trying to get it to sit more comfortably on her head. "And this helmet is going to ruin my hair. I just had it done yesterday."

"Will you all please stop complaining?" Dad said. "Come on—this is going to be fun."

Chaz blew three sharp, shrill blasts on his whistle. He was enjoying the power of having a whistle just a little too much.

"Okay, teams. Line up," Chaz said through his horn. "Does everyone know what the rules are?"

"No," Hannah, Peyton, and I said in unison. Unfortunately, we were drowned out by an enthusiastic chorus of yeses from everyone else, including Dad. One of the other teams—a peppy couple in their seventies who were attending the camp with their children and grandchildren, all of whom were wearing matching purple T-shirts emblazoned with the slogan YES, WE CAN—started cheering so enthusiastically, they drowned out Chaz's last-minute tips.

"What?" Hannah yelled at me.

"I have no idea," I yelled back.

"Three, two, one, GO!" Chaz yelled. He blew his whistle again, and everyone but us began racing toward the first obstacle, which was a rope ladder. The purple team got there first and began scaling up it. We were the last team to arrive, and by the time Peyton, Hannah, and I had walked over, Dad was already at the foot of the rope ladder, waiting impatiently for us.

"Come on, come on," he said.

"Richard, I really don't think I can do this," Peyton said. She looked worriedly up at the ladder.

"Of course you can! Come on—start climbing, girls," Dad said.

Hannah and I both tentatively started to climb. Dad jumped on right behind us, and Peyton slowly brought up the rear. I could hear her swearing under her breath the whole way up. At the top of the ladder there was a platform that connected to another platform via an extremely rickety wooden bridge, which twisted and turned when you stepped on it. The rest of the teams had already scrambled across it and were on to the next challenge, which was a rope swing.

"Is this even safe?" Hannah said, after putting one foot on the bridge to test it and quickly withdrawing it. "What if we fall?"

We both peered down at the ground below, which looked very solid and very hard.

"I think that's what the helmets are for," I said.

"I'd rather have a net," Hannah said.

Peyton arrived on the platform beside us, puffing from the effort.

"Where's Dad?" I asked, surprised that Peyton had made it to the top before my dad had.

Peyton actually smiled, which was unusual for her at the best of times, much less under the current circumstances.

"He's stuck," she said.

We all turned and looked down the rope ladder. Dad's foot was stuck in the rope ladder. He clung to the ropes, red-faced and wild-eyed, while Chaz—who still had the bullhorn tucked under his arm—attempted to untangle him.

"I've never seen anyone manage to get their foot stuck before. How did you do this?" Chaz said, grunting with the effort.

"Go on without me," Dad shouted at us. "We can still win."

Hannah and I looked at one another and were overcome by a fit of the giggles. Even Peyton couldn't resist joining in.

"I'm totally not going over that," Hannah said, pointing at the twisty bridge.

"If we leave now, we can drive to Hawks Cay Resort and see if they have any rooms available," Peyton said.

Hannah and I both cheered this suggestion. The three of us turned and climbed back down the rope ladder, taking care to avoid stepping on my dad.

"What are you doing? You're going the wrong way!" Dad said frantically.

"Mr. Bloom, you have to stop moving around so much if I'm going to get you free," Chaz grunted.

Once Hannah, Peyton, and I were all safely on the ground, we unbuckled and removed our helmets. I hadn't realized how hot my head had been until the helmet was off. I lifted my hair into a ponytail to cool off my neck, while we watched Chaz's continued efforts to free Dad.

"Why don't you take his shoe off," I suggested. "It might be easier to get his foot out."

"I already thought of that," Chaz said, sounding aggrieved. "But his laces are triple knotted. I can't get them to budge."

"I didn't want them to come undone in the middle of the race," Dad explained.

"What are we going to do about Richard?" Hannah asked. "He's not going to want to leave."

"He might, after this," I said.

"He can either come with us, or stay here in his tent. But I'm officially done with camping," Peyton said crisply. "Come on, girls. Let's go pack up the car. Maybe Richard will be free by the time we're ready to go."

Chapter Seventeen

Even though Dad grumbled loudly that we'd hijacked his plans, we ended up having a really nice time during the rest of our stay in the Keys. Peyton booked us into a villa at Hawks Cay Resort, and we spent the weekend lounging by the pool and eating delicious things in air-conditioned restaurants. And even though the trip didn't go exactly as my dad had planned, I thought his goal had been achieved. By the time we arrived back at the beach house in Orange Cove, we might actually all have grown a bit closer together. Peyton had even smiled at me when I teased Dad about getting tangled up in the rope ladder.

As soon as the car was unloaded, Hannah headed to her room, announcing that she had clients she needed to touch base with. I had a weekend's worth of homework to catch up on—and I wanted to do so without constant interruptions from Hannah keeping me updated on how her clients' weekend dates had gone—so I threw my backpack in Bumblebee's trunk and headed to Grounded.

The coffee shop was more crowded than usual with Orange Cove High students, as well as the Geek High crowd. I wasn't the only one who'd gotten the bright idea to study there. Luckily, I was able to get a table by the window. I pulled out my cell phone and called Finn.

He answered his phone with "Yo."

"Have you done the physics homework yet?" I asked.

"What do you think?"

"I think it's highly unlikely that you've done it," I said.

"Ding, ding, ding. We have a winner," Finn said.

"But you're going to do it, right?" I said.

"Doubtful," Finn said. "But I like your optimism."

"Forrester said that he's failing anyone who doesn't maintain at least a C average on their homework," I reminded him.

"Yawn," Finn said.

"Come on. Meet me at Grounded and we can do it together," I said temptingly. Science had never been my strongest class, but Finn always aced it with minimal effort.

"You suck at physics. What's in it for me?" Finn asked.

"My friendship and undying gratitude?" I suggested.

"What else?"

I considered this. "How about a piece of chocolate cake?" I suggested. Grounded had a decadent six-layer chocolate mocha cake with chocolate ganache frosting that Finn was addicted to.

"I want three pieces," Finn said promptly.

"Two," I countered.

"Deal. I'll be there in fifteen minutes."

While I waited for Finn to arrive, I got out my physics book and set up my laptop, and then reviewed the assignment. My heart sank. It was impossibly long and complicated. Maybe I would have to bribe Finn with three pieces of cake in order to get him to help me through it. I started rereading the chapter. Ten minutes later, I heard my name.

"Hi, Miranda."

I looked up. Nora was standing there, smiling down at me.

"Hey, Nora. What are you doing here?" I asked.

"I just talked to Finn. I called him for help with the physics homework, and he said you were meeting over here to go over it. Do you mind if I work with you guys?" Nora asked.

Actually, I did mind a little. I liked Nora, but lately she seemed to be turning up everywhere I went. But I didn't want to be mean by making her feel like she wasn't wanted.

"Not at all," I said.

"Great." Nora smiled, looking relieved. "I tried to do it on my own, but I couldn't figure it out. So I called Finn for help, and he said to come over here. He also said something about his price being a piece of chocolate cake."

"He hit you up for cake, too?" I asked. "What a pig."

Nora sat down and got her things out.

"How was your trip?" she asked.

"It got off to a rocky start, but eventually it was really fun," I said.

I told Nora about the retreat, our aborted attempt at scaling the rope course, and how Peyton, Hannah, and I had revolted and insisted on checking in to a resort.

"So you didn't do any of the other group activities?" Nora asked.

"Nope. We got the heck out of there," I said. "But while we were packing up the car, I heard one of the other families talking about how they had to do some role-playing exercise. They had to pretend to be one another—the mom would pretend to be the son, and the son the mom, for example—and then carry out a conversation that way."

Nora shuddered. "That sounds hideous."

"Yeah, that was pretty much my thought," I said. "They said another team had to cook a meal with just a pot, a spoon, and a can opener. Apparently, it was meant to bring the family closer together through adversity and problem solving. I think we were lucky to escape when we did."

"Was your dad angry that you made him leave?"

"A little, but I don't think he was really prepared to deal with the three of us after two days without pillows, showers, or toilets. It would have gotten very ugly, very quickly," I said. "How was your weekend? Did you and Charlie end up going to West Palm?"

Nora nodded, smiling brightly. "Yeah, it was really great. The exhibit was fantastic."

"I didn't know you were into art," I said.

"Sure, I am. Who doesn't like art?" Nora said.

"Me," Finn said, appearing out of nowhere and plopping down into an empty seat. "I hate art."

"You don't like art?" Nora asked him. "Do you mean modern art? Because some of that can be weird. I don't always get it."

"He doesn't mean it. He just likes saying things he thinks are shocking," I said.

"No, I meant what I said and I said what I meant. I hate art. All art," Finn said. "Except for anime and video games. Does that count?"

"Anime definitely counts," Nora said.

"So you're saying you can't appreciate a landscape by Van Gogh? Or Monet's water lily paintings?" I challenged him.

"What's up with you? Are you channeling Charlie today?" Finn said.

"No. But if Charlie were here and heard you denouncing all art— or all art except for anime and computer graphics—her head would start spinning," I said.

"And she'd start shrieking in such a high-pitched tone, only dogs would be able to hear her," Finn said fondly.

"And she'd call you a philistine," Nora added. Which was a little unexpected, because she didn't really know Charlie all that well. How would Nora know how Charlie would respond?

"Yes, that's our Charlie. She just loves to throw the *p*-word around," Finn said.

"Is Charlie home?" I asked Finn. "She was dog-sitting Willow this weekend. I need to go pick her up."

Finn shrugged. "Who knows? No one told me it was my weekend to keep track of Charlie."

"She's not home," Nora said unexpectedly. "She's on a date."

"She is?" I asked.

Finn straightened in his chair and frowned. "A date? With who?"

Nora shrugged. "I think she said his name was Chad. Does that sound right? Maybe it was Thad."

"It must be Chad," I said.

"No way. You didn't tell me she's still dating that guy," Finn said. He glared at me, as though it were my fault.

"I didn't know she was," I said, shrugging.

Chad was a friend of Dex's. Over the summer, Hannah had set Charlie and Chad up in an attempt to make Finn jealous. At first, the ploy had worked, and Finn *had* been jealous. In fact, he was so freaked out by the sight of Charlie flirting with Chad at the bowling alley that he didn't even notice when Phoebe stormed out. But just when it looked like Hannah's plan was going to be a success, Finn and Phoebe patched things up.

I knew Charlie had gone out on a few dates with Chad, but I hadn't gotten the impression that she was interested in him. Mostly because every time she'd gone out with him, she'd called me afterward and said, "I am *so* not interested in him. I have got to break things off now before he starts getting any ideas about my becoming his girlfriend."

I couldn't help wondering whether Charlie was yet again attempting to make Finn jealous now that he'd broken up with Phoebe.

Bad idea, I thought. *Very bad idea.*

"We should get started on the physics homework," I said.

"I want my cake first," Finn said, still looking grumpy.

"You're seriously going to make us buy you baked goods?" I asked.

"Yes," Finn said. "Yes, I am. I want cake. And if you want help with the homework, you'd better buy some for me."

Nora rolled her eyes at me and stood. "Don't worry. I'll get him the first slice."

"And a mocha latte, too. With extra mocha and extra whipped cream," Finn said.

"Do you want anything?" Nora asked me.

"No, I'm good," I said.

She went off to the counter to order. I turned to Finn.

"What do you think of Nora?" I asked.

"She's cool. Very funny," Finn said.

"She is?" I asked. "I mean, I like her, but I've never really thought of her as particularly funny."

"That's because you've been spoiled by my comedic genius. Everyone else pales in comparison," Finn said.

"I don't think that's it," I said.

"What do you mean?"

"The only time Nora ever jokes around is when she's with you. And when she's around Charlie, she's interested in art," I said. "And when she's with me—" I stopped, considering what Nora and I mostly talked about. "When she's with me, we're both girls who have long-distance boyfriends."

Finn shook his head. "Miranda, Miranda, Miranda," he said sadly.

"What?"

" 'Paranoia strikes deep in the heartland,' " Finn said.

"I don't even know what that means," I said.

"It's a lyric from a Paul Simon song."

"And how, exactly, does that apply to this situation?" I asked. "Are you saying that I'm being paranoid?"

Finn shrugged. "If the lyric fits," he said.

I remembered why I never discussed anything serious with Finn. I should be having this conversation with Charlie instead. In any event, Nora returned then with two mochas and two slices of chocolate cake on a plastic tray.

"One's for you, Finn," Nora said, setting down a plate in front of him. "And, Miranda, I thought you and I could share the other slice."

"Thanks, Nora," I said, feeling incredibly guilty. While I was accusing Nora of being disingenuous, she was buying me cake.

We made a group decision that we should eat our cake to build up our strength before attempting the physics homework. Finn dug into his with gusto, scarfing it down, while Nora and I consumed our piece at a more leisurely pace.

"Is Hannah still mad at me?" Finn asked through a mouthful of chocolate cake.

"I don't know," I said. "She was at first. But she's actually been getting clients through that Web site you designed. And people who really do seem to need her help."

"See? Truth in advertising," Finn said. "It's always the way to go. Has she found any honeys to hook me up with?"

"Not that I know of," I said, thinking how glad I was that Charlie wasn't here to overhear this conversation.

"Tell her to get on it. I need a new girlfriend before Phoebe starts dating someone else," Finn said.

"It's not a contest," I said.

"Of course it is. And I intend to win," Finn said.

"Is your stepsister good at setting people up?" Nora asked.

"She likes to take credit for setting Dex and me up, but he and I already liked each other. She just sort of gave us both a push in the right direction," I said.

"Maybe I should get her to set me up," Nora said thoughtfully.

"What about Marcus?" I asked.

"Oh," Nora said. She reddened, and looked down at our half-eaten piece of cake. "Actually, we broke up."

"You *did*? When?" I asked.

"Over the weekend," Nora said vaguely.

"Why didn't you say anything?" I asked.

"I don't know." She shrugged. "I don't really feel like talking about it."

"That's not very chicklike of you," Finn commented. "I thought all girls did was sit around and talk about their relationships. You know: 'Isn't he cute!' 'Do you think he likes me?' 'Let's talk about our feelings.' That sort of thing."

"I'm so glad you don't fall into the trap of stereotyping people, Finn," I said.

But even as I was rolling my eyes at Finn's ridiculous impersonation of teen girls, part of me sort of agreed with him. Breaking up with a boyfriend *was* a big thing. Why hadn't Nora mentioned it? If Dex and I broke up—and just the thought made my stomach lurch unpleasantly—I certainly wouldn't hide it from my friends.

I decided to try again. "Aren't you upset?"

"Not really. We'd been growing apart for a while, pretty much ever since I left Boston. The long-distance relationship thing was just too hard." She straightened and looked at me directly. "I think that's why I didn't say anything to you about it. I didn't want to freak you out."

"Why would I be freaked out?" I asked.

"You frequently freak out, M," Finn said. "Especially when you've been hitting the lattes too hard. You get wound up tighter than a cheap watch."

"I do not," I said indignantly.

"Yes, you do," Finn said.

I resisted the urge to dump my bottle of water over Finn's head. I decided it was more important to feel Nora out.

"Why would you breaking up with your boyfriend freak me out?" I asked Nora again.

"You know. The whole long-distance relationship not working out. I didn't want you to worry about you and Dex," Nora said.

"I'm not worried," I said.

"Good. Because you totally shouldn't be," Nora said. "Marcus and I were on the verge of breaking up even before I left. I guess my moving away was the last straw."

"But you never said anything about that. In fact, I thought you said that you guys were really tight. You seemed determined to make it work," I said.

Nora shrugged and looked away again. "I think I was just being hopeful. Look, I really don't want to talk about it, okay?"

"Okay," I said.

"Does this mean we're done with the feelings-sharing and relationship portion of the night?" Finn asked. "Good. I can't believe I'm saying this, but I'd rather do the physics homework."

Chapter Eighteen

After I left Grounded, I swung by the Teagues' house to pick up Willow. Charlie wasn't home yet, but her mom was there. Mrs. Teague looked relieved to see me. A weekend's proximity to Willow had left her red-eyed and sniffly.

When Willow and I got back to the beach house, I sent Dex a text, asking him if he wanted to talk on Skype. A moment later, he texted me back, saying he definitely did, but needed five minutes. This was just enough time for me to head to my bedroom and dig my laptop out of my backpack. I had just gotten my computer turned on and pulled up Skype when Dex rang in.

"Hey," he said, grinning broadly. "How was your trip to the Keys?"

"After a few minor setbacks, it was fun," I said. I briefly filled him in on our trip—Dex laughed when I told him about the obstacle course debacle—and then I asked him, "Have you ever had a friend who seemed a little sketchy?"

"What do you mean?" Dex asked.

"I'm not entirely sure," I admitted. "That's the problem. I could just be making something out of nothing."

"Why don't you start at the beginning?" Dex said.

So I told him about Nora, and how we'd become friends.

"I told her about you, and she told me she had a long-distance boyfriend, too," I said. "We bonded over that at first. But then tonight, she said that she and her boyfriend broke up over the weekend. And the way she said it was really weird."

Dex shook his head. "I don't understand. Weird how?"

"This may sound crazy, but I got the feeling that she'd made the whole thing up," I said.

"What? That they broke up?"

"That she even had a boyfriend in the first place," I said.

"Seriously? Why would she make up something like that?" Dex asked.

"I don't know. I don't know that she did," I said, wanting to be fair to Nora. "It's just a feeling I got. She seemed really detached. Most people are upset when they've just gone through a breakup. Even Finn was upset when Phoebe dumped him."

Dex looked unconvinced. I couldn't blame him. My evidence was paper thin.

"There's more," I said. "Nora is . . . is a chameleon. She never once mentioned to me that she was interested in art. But then she found out that Charlie's an artist, and suddenly, when she's with Charlie, that's all she wants to talk about. And then, when she's with Finn, she starts cracking jokes."

"But she's just getting to know all of you, right? Maybe that's just how she makes friends. You know, by finding common ground," Dex said.

"I thought of that. And that could be all it is. It's just . . . I don't know. Something about the way Nora does it pings my radar," I said, feeling frustration build up inside of me. How did I explain that tonight, when I mentioned Marcus to her, I was sure Nora couldn't remember who I was talking about for a few beats? Finn was right; it *did* sound paranoid. But even so, I was sure I was right.

"Take it from me: it's really hard to be the new kid in school," Dex said.

"I know. But you wouldn't make up stories about yourself just to get people to like you," I said.

Dex shrugged.

"You wouldn't," I protested.

"I probably wouldn't make up a whole bunch of stuff, no. But if the guys here were hanging out and shooting the breeze about something, I might act more interested in the topic of conversation than I really was," Dex said.

"I get that. And believe me, that's what I thought Nora was doing at first," I said. "But this goes beyond that."

"Why don't you just take a break?" Dex suggested. "Stop hanging out with her so much. Tell her you're busy with school or *The Ampersand* or whatever."

"I could do that," I said. "But now she's hanging out with Charlie and Finn, too. So whenever I make plans with one of them, Nora suddenly shows up, too. It's like I can't get away from her."

As soon as the words were out of my mouth, I knew how it sounded: like I was jealous of Nora. And, if I was being honest with myself, maybe I was.

"You know what? Forget I said anything," I said, flapping one hand. "I'm sure I'm just blowing this all out of proportion."

"Are you sure you don't want to keep talking about it?"

"Yeah, I'm sure. How was your weekend?"

"It was fine," Dex said.

"What did you do?"

"Same old. Lacrosse practice. Study group," he said. "There was a Monty Python double feature last night in the auditorium. They showed *The Holy Grail* and *Life of Brian*."

"I haven't seen them," I said.

"You have to. They're hilarious," Dex said. He grinned at me. "Wait for me, and I'll watch them with you when I'm home for Thanksgiving break."

"You've got a deal," I said, smiling back at him.

◆

By the time I got off Skype with Dex, I had just about convinced myself that I was completely overreacting. I shut my laptop, then yawned and stretched.

Bedtime, I decided. After the long car trip home, followed by two hours of intensive physics homework, I was beat. Willow was already asleep, snoozing on her big round bed.

I headed down to the kitchen for a glass of water. Hannah was there, leaning against the counter, talking animatedly into her Bluetooth.

"What do you mean the date was a disaster? What happened?" Hannah asked. She frowned, listening intently. "What are you talking about? Corey is totally adorable. You're perfect for each other, Leo."

I wondered who Hannah had set Leo up with. It was clear from Hannah's furrowed brow as she listened to him that Leo wasn't happy about it.

"I think you need to adjust your expectations," Hannah said soothingly. "There are different levels of attractiveness. It's important to figure out which level you're on, and date accordingly."

"Hannah!" I said.

Hannah held up a hand to silence me. I rolled my eyes and poured some water into a glass.

"Remember, you're not necessarily going to fall in love with the first person you go out with," Hannah said. "Why don't we get together tomorrow, and we'll go over your options. Okay? Okay. Great. Bye. Wait, Miranda, don't go."

I'd been on my way to bed, but I stopped at the door and turned back. As much as I hated to admit it, I was itching to hear an update on poor Leo.

"What happened with Leo's date?" I asked.

"Disaster," Hannah admitted. "Definitely not a good match. Poor Corey."

"Why poor Corey?"

"She has an unfortunate excess of body hair," Hannah said delicately. "I tried to talk her into waxing off her mustache, but she was very much against the idea. I don't know why. One second of pain, and *voilà*, the problem is taken care of. Anyway, I didn't think Leo would mind the mustache so much—I mean, let's face it, he's not exactly a perfect physical specimen himself—but I guess he's determined to be picky." Hannah shrugged. "I'll just have to find someone else for him."

"Why don't you ask him if there's anybody at school he's already interested in?" I suggested.

"I did. Every single girl he named is way out of his league. Even worse, I think he might be developing a crush on Avery," Hannah said.

"Avery? Seriously? After she was so mean to him and cut off his hair?"

"Yeah, I know, right? Maybe it's like when victims fall in love with their kidnappers," Hannah said.

"Stockholm Syndrome," I said. "But I think the idea with Stockholm Syndrome is that the victim starts to see their abductor as all-powerful. They exert total control over their victims."

"Exactly. I wouldn't be surprised if that's how Leo sees Avery," Hannah said.

"I've been meaning to ask you, why, exactly, are you hanging out with Avery again?" I asked.

"We're not hanging out. I just thought she'd be a good addition to the business. After all, Avery's really good at making people over. She has a great talent for sizing people up and clearly seeing their flaws," Hannah said.

I just bet she does, I thought. I'd experienced what it was like to have Avery's sharp, critical eyes looking over me. It always made me feel like I had spinach in my teeth and a piece of toilet paper stuck to my shoe.

"But she stole a sweater out of your mom's closet. Do you really want her hanging out at the beach house?" I asked.

"Don't worry. I keep a careful watch on her. And it's purely a professional relationship."

"Why don't you get one of the twins to help you instead," I suggested. Tiffany and Brittany—twin sisters—were friends of Hannah's. They both seemed to know a lot about fashion and makeup.

"I love Tiff and Britt, but let's face it, they're not exactly rocket scientists," Hannah said.

"And Avery is?"

"Avery's actually really smart. And she's very perceptive about people," Hannah said.

I had to admit, I could see her point.

"So, what are you going to do about Leo?" I asked.

"I don't know," Hannah admitted. "Can you think of anyone from your school who might be persuaded to go out with him? A little geekette with a lonely heart and a fondness for short boys with long sideburns?"

"I thought the sideburns were gone," I said.

"For now. But Leo's threatening to grow them back out." Hannah sighed. "Why won't my clients just take my advice? He'd be so much better off if he just listened to me."

I slung an arm around my stepsister's shoulders. "I'm sure all matchmakers wonder the same thing," I said.

Chapter Nineteen

I cornered Charlie the next morning at our lockers before the first bell rang.

"I stopped by your house last night," I said.

"Yeah, my mom told me. I think Willow had fun with her Auntie Charlie," she said. "Did you know that she likes butter pecan ice cream?"

"Willow likes all flavors of ice cream. You didn't give her any, did you? Dairy upsets her stomach," I said.

"That probably explains why she had such bad gas," Charlie said. "She produced some truly horrifying smells."

I had the feeling she was trying to distract my attention. It wasn't going to work.

"What's this I hear about you going out with Chad?" I asked.

"What about it?" Charlie asked. She carefully avoided meeting my eyes as she unloaded the books she'd brought home over the weekend out of her bag and into her locker.

I folded my arms, leaned against the lockers, and waited. After Charlie had dithered as long as possible, she finally closed her locker and turned to me.

"You're not going to make a big deal out of this, are you?" she asked.

"I don't know. Is there something to make a big deal out of?" I asked.

"No! It really wasn't anything," Charlie said. "Chad called and asked if I wanted to go see the new Johnny Depp movie. And I did, so we went."

She closed her locker with an assertive bang.

"And that's it, is it?" I asked. "Finn is newly single, and you just happen to start dating the very same guy you were using before to make Finn jealous? It's all just a coincidence?"

"Yes, it is. And I never used Chad. I just maybe encouraged him a bit more than I otherwise would have," Charlie said.

"Oh, please. Do you really think I'm going to buy that?" I asked.

"You don't have to buy anything. It's really none of your business," Charlie said coolly.

I raised my eyebrows. Charlie relented.

"Okay. So maybe the timing of this date worked out to my advantage," she admitted. "And, by the way? It totally worked. Finn called me last night when I got back from the movies."

"I'm not surprised. He seemed really annoyed when Nora told us you'd gone out with Chad," I said.

Charlie smiled. "Good," she said. "He was pretty worked up about it when I talked to him."

"Why? What did he say?"

"You know, typical Finn stuff. Insulting Chad's intelligence, insulting my taste in guys in general, saying he's pretty sure he saw Chad's photo on *America's Most Wanted*. You know, basically trying to get under my skin," Charlie said, looking pleased with herself.

"Charlie," I said.

"What?"

"You know what I'm going to say," I said.

"If I already know, there's no point in telling me," she said.

"Stop playing games. Tell Finn how you feel," I said.

"No way," Charlie said.

"Yes way. Tell him, and find out if he feels the same way about you. If he does, you guys can finally stop this craziness and just be together. If he doesn't, you can move on," I said.

I'd told Charlie this enough times—and she'd ignored the advice enough times—that I didn't expect her to suddenly agree with me now. So I wasn't surprised when she shook her green head and looked obstinate. Charlie was the most stubborn person I knew.

"Just drop it already, Miranda," she said.

"I just think—" I began. But before I could finish, Nora bounded up.

"Hey, guys," she said enthusiastically. "Charlie, how did it go last night?"

"Which part?" Charlie asked, her face softening into a smile. "The date part, or the part where Finn was totally jealous when he called me after I got home?"

"So it worked! I was hoping it would. I let it sort of just casually slip out about your date," Nora said.

"Excellent job," Charlie said. She and Nora slapped hands.

I just stood there, looking from Charlie to Nora and back to Charlie again as they chatted animatedly about the details of Charlie's date with Chad and the phone conversation she'd had with Finn afterward. I knew Nora had guessed that Charlie had feelings for Finn, but I was surprised that Charlie had confided in Nora. She'd been paranoid about anyone knowing. In fact, up until now, the only people she'd told were me and Hannah.

I couldn't help it—the now-familiar flash of jealousy shot through me. I went away for one weekend, and suddenly Charlie and Nora were best friends? Going to museums and sharing secrets?

I grabbed my backpack off the ground and slung it over one shoulder.

"I have to get to class," I said.

Nora and Charlie looked up, startled out of their confidence sharing.

"The bell's about to ring," I said.

Charlie checked her watch. "Miranda's right. I should get to class. I'll tell you the rest of it later, Nora."

"Yeah, tell me at lunch," Nora said.

"No, not at lunch. Finn will be there," Charlie said. "We'll go to Grounded after school."

"Great," Nora said.

I waited for one of them to invite me along to Grounded, too, but neither of them did. Instead, they said their good-byes, and then Nora turned to me and said, "Come on, we'd better go. We're going to be late for lit class."

"Right. We wouldn't want to be late," I said, wondering if I sounded as sour as I felt.

◆

My day didn't get better. In fact, it only got worse.

I had to endure physics class, then lunch, with friction at an all-time high between Charlie and Finn. Actually, it was pretty one-sided. The more Finn sulked and tried to goad Charlie into sparring with him, the more pleased with herself Charlie seemed. And Charlie and Nora kept exchanging meaningful looks, as if this was all exactly the reaction they'd been hoping for when they cooked up their little scheme. I just sat there stewing and feeling completely left out.

Then, just before last period, Candace Ruckman tracked me down.

"Miranda, I need to talk to you about your story," Candace said.

I could tell from the way she was glowering at me—round blue eyes disdainful, pink-glossed lips pursed, arms crossed—that she had not sought me out to shower my article with praise. My heart sank. I thought I'd done a good job.

"What's wrong with it?" I asked nervously.

"Is it true that the guy you interviewed for that piece is your boyfriend?" Candace asked.

She was, as usual, perfectly pressed—today's wrinkle-free outfit was a striped oxford shirt tucked into skinny white jeans—which made her even more foreboding.

I nodded. "Is that a problem?"

"Yes, it's a problem!" Candace said. "It's a breach of journalistic ethics!"

"It is?" I bleated. "Why?"

"Because you did a complete profile on this guy without disclosing that you have a personal relationship with him. That's completely unacceptable," Candace said. "You're lucky it was just a profile and not a news piece, which would have been far worse. Anyway, we can't run it. I'm cutting it from the issue."

My first real publishing credit was slipping away. I made a desperate attempt to grab it back.

"But I could add a disclosure," I said. "I'll just put a paragraph in the beginning saying that I know Dex. Besides, does it really matter? Like you said, it's not a news piece. Just a profile. My knowing Dex doesn't make it less interesting."

Candace shook her head. "*The Ampersand* may be a high school magazine, but I still expect all of my writers to conform to the highest standards of professional journalism. And that certainly does not include doing a profile on your boyfriend and adding in a sloppy, after-the-fact disclaimer."

My cheeks were burning hot and red. I couldn't believe it. I'd worked so hard on my article. Not only had it not impressed Candace, but it had actually made me lose credibility with her.

"Are you kicking me off the magazine staff?" I asked. My mouth felt very dry, and my tongue felt large and unwieldy.

"No. But I'm also not going to give you a new assignment for the second issue. Instead I want you to redo your student-athlete piece," Candace said. She cocked her head to one side, and her eyes softened. "You know, your concept was good. I like the idea of the profile. You just need to find someone to interview who isn't your boyfriend."

I nodded, my face still flaming. "I understand," I said.

"Good." Candace turned, as if to leave.

"Wait . . . Candace?" I asked.

She looked back at me. "Yes?"

"Who told you that Dex is my boyfriend?" I asked.

Candace frowned, clearly not sure why I was wasting her time with such questions. But then she shrugged and said, "That new girl on layout. What's her name again? Nora, I think. Nora Lee."

Chapter Twenty

As I walked out of school to the student parking lot, my head buzzed with anger. Why had Nora told Candace that Dex was my boyfriend? Had she deliberately set out to sabotage me? And, if so, why? Had she known from the time she spent working on the student newspaper at her old school that telling Candace would get me in trouble?

I took a few deep, cleansing breaths, and tried to talk myself out of jumping to conclusions. Especially such far-flung, paranoid conclusions. Maybe Nora just mentioned my relationship with Dex in passing, not realizing that Candace would have a problem with my interviewing him for my story. After all, I hadn't known I was doing anything wrong. So how would Nora?

By the time I reached Bumblebee, I had calmed down somewhat. I just needed to talk to Nora, to hear her side of the story. Remembering that Nora and Charlie had made plans to meet at Grounded after school—the fact that they hadn't invited me along, too, still stung—I decided to drive straight there and talk to Nora immediately. Before my anger and suspicions had time to fester.

When I walked through the glass front door of Grounded, I saw Nora and Charlie sitting at a table in the back, their heads bowed close together, deep in conversation. They didn't notice me until I was standing right at their table, towering over them. Then Charlie looked up.

"Hey, Miranda," she said, surprised.

"Hey," I said. I glanced at Nora, and thought that for just a fraction of a second, I saw a flicker of annoyance pass over her face. But a moment later, it was gone—replaced by a welcoming smile—and I wondered if I'd imagined it.

"Hi, Miranda," Nora said. "Have a seat. Or are you going to get a coffee first?"

"I didn't know you were going to be here," Charlie said.

"I didn't, either," I said. "But something happened that I need to talk to Nora about."

I sat down across from Nora and tried to think of how I should begin. I didn't want to sound like I was accusing her of anything. *Maybe I should have practiced what I was going to say on the drive over*, I thought.

"I just talked to Candace. She's pulling my article from the first issue of *The Ampersand*," I said.

"What? Why?" Charlie asked, frowning.

I looked at Nora, watching her reaction. And, unless I was very much mistaken, Nora wasn't surprised by this news. Not one little bit. My suspicions flared a little higher.

"What, exactly, did Candace say?" Nora asked.

"She said that it was unethical for me to write the profile without disclosing that Dex is my boyfriend," I said.

"Really? Is that true?" Charlie asked.

"Apparently. I didn't know that, of course, or I would have disclosed it. Or written about something else," I said.

"Of course," Charlie said. "So how did Candace find out that you and Dex are dating?"

"She said Nora told her," I said, looking straight at Nora.

For a moment, Nora's face was an absolute blank. It was as though she hadn't even heard me. But then, as if she'd reached a decision, she finally nodded once and arranged her features into an expression of concern.

"I did tell her that," Nora said. "I'm so sorry, Miranda. I didn't know it would get you into trouble."

There is something going on here, I thought. Something sketchy about the way she was reacting that made my Spidey-sense tingle.

"Why did you tell Candace that Dex is my boyfriend?" I asked, taking care to keep my voice neutral.

Charlie gave me an odd, searching look. "I'm sure Nora didn't mean anything by it," she said.

I continued to look at Nora.

"It just sort of came out," Nora said.

"How did it sort of come out?" I asked.

"I don't remember exactly. I was in *The Ampersand* office, working on layout, and I saw that Candace was editing your piece. And I knew how hard you had worked on it, so I couldn't help myself—I asked her if she had liked it. And she said that she thought it was an interesting angle, and wondered aloud how you'd found Dex. And I just sort of blurted it out. That he was your boyfriend," Nora said.

"And what did Candace say?" I asked.

Nora looked down at her coffee cup resting on the table. She had both hands wrapped around it, as though she were warming them.

"She seemed pretty ticked off about the whole thing," Nora admitted. "She might have said something about it being unethical."

I looked at Nora with what I hoped was a cool, level gaze. Because at the moment, I didn't feel at all calm. Instead, my head was buzzing again, as though a swarm of angry bees had taken up residence inside my skull.

"Why didn't you tell me?" I asked.

Charlie was frowning, her head cocked to one side, as she looked from me to Nora and back again.

"I was going to," Nora said. "But . . ." She trailed off.

"But what?" I prompted her.

"I was afraid you'd be mad at me," Nora said in a small voice. She seemed to become physically smaller, too. She folded up on herself, crossing her legs and arms, her shoulders slumping forward, her chin drooping.

"Miranda's not mad at you," Charlie assured her. "Are you Miranda?"

Oh yes, I am, I wanted to say, feeling a flicker of annoyance at Charlie for taking Nora's side. Charlie was supposed to be *my* best friend, after all. Didn't she see that something hinky was going on here?

"I don't understand why you didn't warn me, so I'd be prepared when Candace talked to me about it," I said.

Nora shook her head helplessly. "I'm really sorry," she said.

"It's fine," Charlie told her. "It was just an accident. You didn't mean for it to happen."

"No, I really didn't. I swear, Miranda," Nora said.

"So, what did Candace say to you?" Charlie asked me.

"Just what Nora said. Basically that interviewing Dex without disclosing my relationship with him was a breach of journalistic ethics," I said.

Charlie rolled her eyes. "Please. The article is for a high school magazine, not the *New York Times*. Don't you think she's overreacting just a bit?"

"Totally overreacting," Nora agreed. "And it was a profile,

right? Not a news piece. Why can't you just say at the beginning how you know Dex? Or you could work it into the body of the article."

"I offered to do that," I admitted. "But Candace said no. It's like she thinks the piece is tainted or something."

"That chick is so uptight," Charlie said. "What happens now?"

"Candace is giving me a second chance to write a student-athlete piece. She liked the idea of my doing a profile, although obviously I can't write about Dex again. I'll have to think of something else. The bad news is that I won't get a shot at a better assignment for the second issue. And I won't have a piece in the first issue," I said.

"You're not the only one," Nora said.

"What do you mean?" I asked.

Nora leaned forward, eyes glowing. "When I was in the *Ampersand* office, I overheard Candace telling one of the guys on the staff that she's spiking Tabitha Stone's short story. That's just how she said it. *Spiking*," Nora said.

This piece of gossip was juicy enough to distract me from my personal plight.

"Seriously?" I asked. "Why?"

"Candace said it was terrible. Whatever Tabitha wrote was all postmodern and nonsensical. There weren't any characters or any sort of a plot. Apparently, there was a paragraph in the middle where she just repeated the word *desolation* over and over again," Nora said.

She was grinning now, and I couldn't help smiling, too. Tabitha Stone was so full of herself, so sure that she was some sort of literary whiz. Maybe this setback would let out some of her hot air.

"Desolation?" I said. "You mean, that was part of the story? How, exactly?"

"That's just it. It wasn't. It was just the word repeated. *Desolation. Desolation. Desolation*," Nora droned.

"But that doesn't make any sense," I said.

"I know. That's what Candace said, too. She actually seemed really annoyed about the whole thing. She said that she'd been clear that she wanted an actual short story, with a plot and characters."

"I really hate it when people have preconceived notions of art. Why does a short story have to have a plot and characters?" Charlie said.

"Because that's the definition of a short story?" I suggested.

"Maybe a paragraph on desolation is central to Tabitha's theme. And why shouldn't it be? It's fascist to dictate art," Charlie said.

"No, it's not. When the result is Tabitha Stone getting her short story spiked, it's great," I said with relish.

"You know what? You should submit one of your short stories, Miranda," Charlie suggested.

"What? No way," I said.

"Why not? They need a short story, and you've written tons of them. It's the perfect solution," Charlie said.

"I don't have one prepared," I protested.

"You have notebooks full of them," Charlie said.

"But nothing I've written is ready for submission," I argued. "For one thing, they're all handwritten. I'd have to find one I like, shape it up, and then type the whole thing out. And I'd probably have to do it immediately, before Candace gives the fiction slot to someone else."

"So? You could totally do that," Charlie said.

"You definitely could," Nora agreed.

Could I? I wondered. Was it possible?

"But would Candace be willing to consider me? Especially after the debacle with my Dex article," I said nervously.

Nora groaned. "I'm so sorry, Miranda. This is all my fault. I really didn't mean to get you in trouble with Candace."

My anger at Nora, which had softened with the excellent gossip about Tabitha Stone's rejected story, now disappeared altogether. She really did seem genuinely sorry.

"It's okay," I said. "I know you didn't mean to."

"I really had no idea she'd react the way she did," Nora said.

"I think Charlie's right. Candace is really uptight. Have you ever noticed that her clothes never, ever wrinkle? I mean, how is that possible?" I said, and was rewarded by a grateful smile from Nora.

"Are you going to submit a story or what?" Charlie asked, leaning forward and resting her head on her fisted hands.

"You totally should," Nora said.

"I don't know," I said. "It's a long shot. And I don't want to come off looking stupid."

"If you're going to be an artist, you have to be fearless, Miranda," Charlie advised.

"Fearless?" I repeated.

"That's right. *Fearless*," Charlie said. "Trust me. It's the only way to go."

Chapter Twenty-one

I decided to follow Charlie's advice. I would be fearless. As soon as I got home from Grounded, I went straight to my room and dug out all of my writing notebooks. I paged through one after another, looking for the perfect short story. Finally, I came across one I'd written months ago.

The story was called "The Traveler." It was about a girl who was adopted at birth and ends up meeting her biological mother on an overseas flight. I'd written it last Christmas, when I was flying back to Orange Cove after visiting my mom in London. I'd gotten the inspiration for the story midflight, and skipped the in-flight movies to scribble it down while the idea was still fresh. I'd struggled a bit with not wanting it to all be too convenient—would the mother and daughter really just happen to end up sitting next to each other on an airplane? What were the odds? But then I decided to solve the problem by having the mother notice the girl in the waiting area prior to the flight and feel an immediate, almost haunting connection to her. So the biological mother arranges to switch seats to be next to the girl once the flight takes off.

As I read the story over, I could see the potential. This was exactly the sort of fiction piece they ran in *The Ampersand*. It was poignant and intriguing, and it had a plot. A good plot, I thought. In fact, I even started to feel a little excited at the potential.

I have to be fearless, I told myself. *Fearless.*

And then I dug out my laptop and set it up on my desk. If I was going to edit and type the story up by tomorrow, I had a lot of work to do.

*

My mom called just before dinner. I'd already been working for a few hours, so I was ready to take a break. Plus, I hadn't talked to my mom in over a week.

"Hello, darling, it's me," Sadie said. My mother had always insisted that I call her by her name. It was part of the weirdness that was Sadie. "What's going down?"

"What's going down?" I repeated. "Are you trying to be hip again? Because if so, you should really give it up. You're too old to be hip."

"Bite your tongue. I am the embodiment of hip," Sadie said. "As you would be, if you'd come to live with me in the bustling metropolis of London, instead of staying in that tiny hick town."

"I like this tiny hick town," I said.

"Tell me all of your news," Sadie said. "And don't leave anything out."

"Well, something actually did happen today," I said, hesitating. It was hard admitting my very first *Ampersand* assignment was a failure.

"What? Wait, don't tell me. Let me guess. Your stepmother had a horrible reaction to her monthly BOTOX injection and her face is now swollen up like a Cabbage Patch Kid's," Sadie said with enthusiasm. Sadie and Peyton had never gotten along very well. "Or she finally decided to start eating carbohydrates, and immediately swelled up to the size of a baby whale."

"No. Not even close," I said.

"Don't keep me in suspense," Sadie said.

I told Sadie all about how the profile I'd written wasn't going to make it into *The Ampersand*, how Candace was annoyed with me for not disclosing that I knew Dex, and how I was planning to submit a short story for the newly open fiction spot in the magazine.

"So if I can convince Candace to read my short story, who knows? Maybe she'll like it," I said.

"That's a wonderful idea, darling. But how did your editor find out that you and Dex are dating? Did you tell her?" Sadie asked.

"No. My friend Nora told her. Accidentally," I added quickly.

"Hmmm," Sadie said.

"What?"

"People rarely do things accidentally," Sadie said. "Who is this Nora? I don't recognize the name."

"That's because you don't know her. Nora's new this year. She moved here from Boston," I said.

"And why was she talking to your editor about your relationship with your boyfriend?" Sadie asked. "That sounds fishy to me."

"It did to me, too, at first," I admitted. "But from the way Nora tells it, I think it really did just slip out. And how could she have known it would end up getting my piece pulled?"

"Well, at the very least, I think she would have been aware that it wouldn't make you look good. Whatever gave you the idea to profile Dex, anyway?" Sadie asked. "That wasn't a very bright idea."

"Actually," I said slowly, "now that you mention it, I think Nora was the one who first suggested it." I remembered now. It was the first time she'd come over to the beach house. I had just gotten the assignment, and was fretting that I didn't know any athletes. And Nora had said, "Isn't your boyfriend an athlete? Why don't you interview him?" To Sadie, I said, "But, seriously, she was just trying to be helpful."

"Hmmm," Sadie said again.

"But I agreed it was a good idea. I didn't know it was against the rules. And I couldn't think of anything better," I said.

"I think that's just your nerves talking," Sadie said. "You were anxious about doing a good job on this assignment so you'd get a better one the next time around. I keep telling you, you have to have more confidence in yourself."

"Charlie calls it being fearless," I said.

"That's the perfect word. It's the only way to go through life, darling. You have to be fearless. Just like me," Sadie said.

It was true. My mother could be narcissistic, selfish, vain. But she was confident in herself. It was something I'd always admired about her.

Sadie continued. "I'm concerned about this Nora person."

"Why? You've never met her," I said. "You don't know anything about her."

"I think I do," Sadie said. "Or I know the type. First, she talks you into focusing your article on Dex. Which, really, darling, was a truly terrible idea."

"Yes, thank you, I'm aware of that now. Do we have to keep talking about it?" I asked.

Sadie ignored me. "And then she goes behind your back and rats you out to your editor. It sounds to me like she set you up. In fact, she reminds me of a character that appeared in one of my books. Everyone thought she was a pious young widow. And in the end she turned out to be a criminal mastermind who had murdered her husband and was getting rich blackmailing members of the aristocracy."

"Mom," I said, in my exasperation forgetting to call her Sadie. "First of all, we're modern-day high school students, not members of the eighteenth-century English aristocracy. And, more important, Nora is a real person, not a character in a novel."

"Art often imitates life, and vice versa" Sadie said darkly. "All I'm saying is that I think you should watch your back."

"Okay," I said.

"Promise me, darling," Sadie insisted.

"Fine. I promise. I'll watch my back," I said, although I rolled my eyes heavenward. Sadie could be such a drama queen.

"And maybe you should keep your distance from this Nora girl. I'm not saying you have to cut her off entirely, but maybe just take it slowly. Don't let her get too close too quickly," Sadie continued.

"That's funny. That's almost exactly what Dex said," I said.

"I knew I liked that boy," Sadie said.

"There's just one thing," I said.

"What's that?"

I shifted the phone from one ear to the other.

"What if Nora's not the problem? What if I'm the problem?" I said.

"You? You've never been a problem. Except when you were a toddler and refused to use the potty. I thought you'd still be in diapers when you started kindergarten," Sadie said.

"Can we please stay on topic?" I said, collapsing back on the pillows piled high against my headboard.

"Of course. What were we talking about again?"

"I was saying, what if the problem isn't with Nora, but with me?" I asked again.

"How so?"

"I've been jealous of her," I admitted. "I'll see Nora with Charlie or Finn, and I feel . . . well, threatened, I guess. And that's not the only time I feel jealous. It also happens with Dex. I wonder about the girls he's meeting at his new school. I hate that I get jealous, but I can't seem to help it."

"It's normal to feel jealous from time to time," Sadie said. "And I'm certainly not a fan of repressing your feelings. If you feel the occasional twinge of jealousy, you should just acknowledge it, feel it deeply, and move on. The problem comes when you let those feelings take over too much of your life."

"But how do you keep that from happening?" I asked.

"The thing is, I don't think it's all that different from what we were talking about earlier. It's all a matter of confidence. You have to have confidence in yourself. And you have to trust your friends, that they can spend time with other people and still love and respect you. And trust that Dex cares about you even when he's away at school."

Sadie's words were comforting, even though I wasn't entirely sure I bought what she was saying. Sure, having self-confidence was a good thing. But it couldn't change reality. If Charlie did decide to make Nora her new best friend, or if Dex decided to break up with me and start dating someone at his new school, no amount of self-confidence could change that.

"It sounds a little New Agey," I said. "Power of positive thinking, and all that."

"I think the power of positive thinking has been misunderstood. The idea isn't that you can change reality by beaming your brain waves at a problem. It's all in how *you* react to a situation. And if you react in a positive, self-loving way, well, then, that can turn things around to your advantage," Sadie said.

I thought about this. Scarily enough, Sadie was starting to make sense to me.

Chapter Twenty-two

I got to school early on Tuesday morning and headed straight to *The Ampersand* office. No one was there, so I dithered for a few minutes, trying to decide what to do. I'd hoped I could hand my short story to Candace in person, so that I could express my enthusiasm to her. But I also wanted to make sure she got the story as soon as possible, and I knew that she checked her mail folder in *The Ampersand* office throughout the day. Finally, I decided it was better to get it into her hands quickly, and then hopefully I'd see her at some point during the day—in between classes, or maybe at lunch—and I'd be able to talk to her then. So I wrote a brief note of explanation, paper clipped it to the short story, and stuck it in Candace's mailbox.

Nora wasn't in lit class that day. I wondered whether she was home sick, and sent her a text message checking up on her. This wasn't exactly keeping the distance my mother had advocated, but I thought a text message was pretty harmless.

"Where's Nora?" Charlie asked when I saw her in physics. The table next to ours, which Nora usually occupied, was empty. Finn wasn't there either, but I'd already seen him at school that morning—it was hard to miss the tall guy with the Mohawk—and so I figured he was just running late, as usual.

"I don't know. I sent her a text earlier, but she never responded," I said.

"I hope she's okay," Charlie said.

"I'm sure she's fine," I said. I hesitated, but then remembered what Sadie had said about having enough self-confidence to trust my friends. "You know, you hurt my feelings yesterday."

"I did?" Charlie looked surprised. "When? How?"

"When you and Nora made plans to meet at Grounded right in front of me and didn't invite me along, too," I said.

"I'm sorry, Miranda," Charlie said. And she really did look sorry, too. "You're right; that wasn't very cool. I just . . ." She stopped and looked down at her hands.

"What?" I asked.

Charlie gestured for me to lean closer, so that we could talk privately, without Tate Metcalf overhearing.

"I think I just got carried away that someone else was excited about the idea of Finn and I getting together," Charlie whispered.

I sat back. "Charlie!" I said at full volume. "How can you think I wouldn't be excited about that?"

"Shhhhh," Charlie said, making frantic throat-slashing gestures.

"Sorry," I said. I leaned back in so I could whisper. "I am completely supportive of you guys getting together. I just don't think you should play games."

"Even if games are what works?" Charlie asked.

I shrugged. "You already know what I think about that," I said.

"That's why I wanted to talk to Nora about it," Charlie said.

"Because she'll just agree with you, no matter what?" I said.

"Is that what you think of her?" Charlie asked, looking surprised. "That she'll just go along with whatever I say?"

"Yeah, maybe," I said, shrugging.

"That's pretty harsh, Miranda," Charlie said. She frowned.

Before I could respond, Finn came in. He was walking oddly, dipping down low into each long step.

"What are you doing?" I asked.

"I'm trying out a new walk," Finn announced. "What do you think? Is it better than my old walk?"

"It's finally happened: Finn has lost his mind," Charlie said.

"How does Chaddy-boy walk? Wait, let me guess." Finn let his face slacken into a dumb, glazed expression and slumped down so that his arms were dragging on the ground, baboon style.

Charlie rolled her eyes. "As if," she said.

"I'm Chad. I can walk and scratch myself at the same time," Finn grunted, demonstrating by scratching his bottom.

"Wow, you're so funny," Charlie said. "*Not.*"

Finn straightened up, and loped over to his seat. Finn never sat down like a normal person. Instead, he always threw himself into his seat, long legs sprawled out in front of him. He turned around to face Charlie and me.

"Hey, Miranda," he said. "Do you have any secret boyfriends I don't know about?"

"No, just the one boyfriend. And he's not a secret," I said.

"Good. That's good. Because it's important for friends to be open and honest with one another, don't you think?" Finn said solemnly.

"I don't have a secret boyfriend," Charlie said. "I just went out on a date. One date does not a boyfriend make."

"Did you ask your stepsister if she has any hotties she can set me up with?" Finn asked me, pointedly ignoring Charlie.

"No. Besides, I don't know if Hannah is in the hottie business. You sort of undermined that part of her business when you posted that Web site advertising for losers to call her," I reminded him.

"Hmmm. Maybe I didn't think that through well enough," Finn said. "Of course, I had a hot girlfriend at the time, so I didn't know I'd be in the market."

"Maybe you should try to find someone to go out with who you like for who she is, rather than what she looks like," I suggested. "Someone you know from school. Someone you can talk and laugh with."

Charlie kicked me sharply in the ankle. I yelped in pain.

"Sorry," Charlie said. "My foot slipped."

Finn gave her a curious look. But just then, the bell rang and Mr. Forrester stood, ending conversation. But as I got my laptop set up, prepared to take notes, I couldn't help smiling to myself. I thought Finn might finally be catching on.

*

As soon as I arrived at *The Ampersand* office for the weekly after-school meeting, I looked for Candace. She wasn't in her usual place at the table at the front of the room. I hadn't seen her all day, and so still hadn't had a chance to talk to her about the short story. *Did she have a chance to read it?* I wondered. My stomach wriggled with nerves.

Be fearless, I reminded myself, and I took a few deep breaths to settle my nerves.

Then, to my surprise, I saw Nora sitting at a table in the middle of the room.

"Hey," I said, sitting next to her. "Where have you been all day? Did you get my text?"

"There was something I had to do," Nora said.

"So you just cut your classes?" I asked. "They don't really let you get away with that here. Someone from the main office will call your grandmother."

"So? She won't care," Nora said.

She seemed to be in an odd mood. I couldn't quite place it—was she upset? Distracted?—but then, suddenly, I realized what it was. Nora wouldn't meet my eyes. In fact, she seemed to be looking just about everywhere except at me. At the whiteboard, where someone had written out a to-do list for Issue One. At Peter Rossi and Coleen Duchene—or, at least, at the back of their heads—who were sitting at the table in front of us, poring over their editorial notes. At Padma, who was hitting the hulking old copier, trying to convince it to spit out her copies.

What's going on? I wondered.

"Nora, is everything okay?" I asked. But then, before she could answer, I heard Candace's voice. I turned quickly, and saw that she had just walked into the office, Jimmy Torres panting at her heels. Jimmy was clearly infatuated with our editor in chief. I wanted to tell him not to waste his time. Candace was way, way out of Jimmy's league.

As I watched, Candace seemed to be gently but firmly trying to get away from Jimmy. Her cool, firm smile was in place, and she was gesturing toward an empty chair, clearly suggesting that he go sit in it. I decided that now was as good a time as any to approach her. Candace might even be grateful to me for giving her a good excuse to get away from Jimmy.

"Wait, hold on one second," I said to Nora. I stood, took a deep breath, and headed up to the front of the room, where Candace was now setting her things down on her table. Jimmy hadn't yet taken the hint. He continued to hover nearby.

". . . and then I was working on my article, and I thought of this killer idea of adding a sidebar to the article. What do you think?" Jimmy was saying.

"Hi, Candace," I said. "Can I talk to you?"

Candace glanced up, and I thought she looked relieved to see me standing there. "Sure, Miranda. Jimmy, give us a minute, please."

Jimmy shot me a resentful glance, but obediently moved back to take the empty seat next to Peter Rossi.

"What's up?" Candace asked. She had this way of standing very still when you spoke to her, which made it seem as though all of her attention was focused directly on you. It was both flattering and unnerving.

Be fearless, I reminded myself.

"Did you get the short story I put in your mail folder this morning?" I asked.

"Yes, I did. I was a bit surprised to get it, actually. You've never mentioned that you're interested in writing fiction," she said.

That just goes to show why you should have confidence in yourself, I thought. *How will anyone ever know what you want if you're not brave enough to stand up and ask for it?*

"I am really interested in fiction. In fact, I write all the time. Mostly short stories, although over the summer I expanded one of my stories into a novella. And I'd . . . well, I'd really love to have one of my stories published in *The Ampersand*. If you think they're good enough, I mean," I said, completely aware that I was babbling, yet completely unable to stop.

"I'll keep that in mind. And I appreciate your enthusiasm," Candace said. She smiled at me and checked her watch. "We should get the meeting started. We have a lot to go over today." Candace raised her voice to be heard over the din. "Everyone, can you take your seats so we can get to work?"

I felt like I'd been slapped. My cheeks flaming, I turned and headed back to my seat. What had just happened? Had Candace read my story? *If so, she must not have liked it very much*, I thought miserably. *If she had, she wouldn't have dismissed me like that.*

I sat next to Nora.

"What did Candace say?" Nora asked, looking straight at me for the first time.

"Nothing really," I said, shrugging helplessly.

Nora nodded, and suddenly became incredibly interested in examining her nails. But I was too busy reliving what had just happened with Candace to wonder about Nora's odd behavior.

Candace held up a hand until everyone had quieted and trained their attention on her. "First off, there have been a few changes in the selection of articles for the first issue. Miranda's student-athlete profile is going to be bumped to the second issue."

Everyone glanced in my direction. My face felt like it was on fire.

"And second, the fiction piece has been reassigned," Candace said.

It was my turn to look around. Tabitha Stone wasn't there. I wondered how she'd responded to having her piece spiked. Would she stay on the magazine staff or resign in a huff? *I wouldn't be at all surprised if Tabitha's massive ego can't handle the rejection*, I thought.

"Luckily, we have among us another literary talent who has submitted a story we're going to use instead. And, I have to tell you, her short story absolutely blew me away," Candace said. "I can honestly say, this is one of the strongest pieces I've ever read. I'm really excited that it's going into our first issue."

I froze. Could she possibly mean . . . Was she talking about . . . Oh, my gosh. Did she mean *me*? *My* short story? My heart started to pound so fast and so hard, it felt like it might burst right out of my chest. Why hadn't she said anything to me about it?

But then Candace continued. "Please join me in congratulating Nora Lee on her amazing short story. I know this is a bit of an unusual decision, as Nora isn't a member of our writing staff. But I think when you read the story, you'll understand why I had to include the piece."

There was some scattered applause mixed in with low murmurings.

"Thank you," Nora said. "I'm really excited to have the opportunity."

I couldn't look at her. In fact, I couldn't move. In an instant, I'd gone from flushing hot with embarrassment to feeling like my entire body had been dipped in ice, freezing me in place.

Nora had submitted a short story to Candace.

No. It was *worse*. Nora had gone behind my back and submitted a short story to Candace.

Nora had sat there, while Charlie urged me to submit one of my own stories, and hadn't said a word about the fact that she was planning on submitting a story of her own.

And Candace had chosen her story over mine.

And suddenly, every single suspicious thought I'd had about Nora came into sharp focus. She *had* copied my clothes. She *had* tried to take over my friends. And now she'd succeeded in snatching the fiction spot on *The Ampersand*.

"Miranda?" Nora said, taking care to keep her voice low, as Candace had moved on to talk about the pressing issues she was having with the layout. "I was going to tell you. I just . . ." Her voice trailed off.

I finally turned to look at her. Nora's face was pale, but otherwise unreadable.

"I just didn't want you to be mad at me," Nora said.

I drew in a deep breath. I was distantly aware that my hands were shaking. I clasped them together under the table.

"Too late," I said.

Chapter Twenty-three

Somehow I managed to get through the rest of the staff meeting sitting next to Nora, even though she was the last person I wanted to be anywhere near at the moment. Even worse, I had to keep my anger contained—I didn't want Candace or anyone else to think I was being a sore loser, in the mold of Tabitha Stone—even though keeping it inside made me feel nauseated.

When the meeting was finally, mercifully, over, I packed up my things immediately, hoping that no one noticed how my hands were still shaking. I thought Nora might try to stop me, to try to talk to me again, but before she could, a small group of staffers led by Candace converged on her. They all wanted to congratulate Nora and discuss her short story. Not wanting to hear another word about how marvelous Nora was, I left quickly.

I drove home, my head buzzing. Unfortunately, Bumblebee didn't have a radio—my dad had considered this a selling point when he bought the car—so I couldn't distract myself with music. But it probably wouldn't have worked, anyway. Nora's betrayal was too enormous for that.

No one was at the beach house when I got home. I was glad. I let Willow out for a potty break and then went to my room, closed the door, and lay down on my bed, staring up at the ceiling fan, which was rotating in lazy circles.

Why did Nora do it? I wondered. Why had she gone behind my back and submitted her story, even after encouraging me to submit mine? She'd never, not once, mentioned that she wrote, too, and she'd had plenty of opportunities.

I tried to channel Charlie and look at the situation in a light that would most favor Nora. Maybe Nora had always dreamed of being a writer, too, and saw this as her big chance to get published. Maybe she'd been working on her story for weeks, or months, even, and didn't want to tell anyone—tell me—about it until it was finished.

The only problem with that scenario was that I just didn't believe it. Nora had already proven herself to be a chameleon. Around Charlie, she was into art. When she with Finn, she suddenly liked video games. With me, she first had a long-distance boyfriend and then—when that story didn't hold together—now she suddenly wanted to be a writer. In fact, it wasn't so much that Nora wanted to be like me. It was more like she wanted to take over my life.

My door opened, and Hannah breezed in.

"Hey," she said. "I saw your car parked out front, but you're so quiet back here, I couldn't tell if you were home."

"I'm home," I said. "Just thinking."

Hannah gave me a strange look. "What's going on? You seem weird. Did something happen? Is it Dex?"

"No, everything with Dex is fine," I said.

"When was the last time you talked to him?" Hannah asked.

"Last night. But for only a few minutes. He had a study group meeting, and I"—I swallowed back the bitter taste in my mouth—"I was working on a short story for *The Ampersand*, so I didn't have time to talk."

"Okay, just spit it out," Hannah said.

"Spit what out?"

"What's going on? You look like you just lost your best friend. Which I know is impossible, because I'm right here," Hannah said. She flopped down on the end of my bed.

This statement startled me right out of my funk. I knew we'd grown a lot closer over the past year, but I had no idea that Hannah thought of me as her best friend. I was touched.

"That's so nice," I said.

Hannah waved a hand at me. "I know, but I don't want to get all sappy right now. Just tell me what's going on."

"It's Nora," I said.

"Your friend?" Hannah asked.

"Ex-friend," I corrected her.

"Uh-oh. What did she do?" Hannah said.

"She's trying to take over my life," I said. Then, realizing that this probably sounded dramatic, I said, "Seriously. She's already taken over my friends. Now she's trying to take over my spot on *The Ampersand*."

"I'm going to need details," Hannah said.

So I started at the beginning and told her everything, even the stuff that made me sound paranoid. I told her about Nora's chameleon behavior, how I was fairly sure she had completely made up an imaginary boyfriend, and how she had swooped in and snagged the fiction spot in the first issue of *The Ampersand*. Hannah listened quietly and attentively, not once interrupting to tell me that it sounded far-fetched.

Finally, when I'd finished, I looked at Hannah. "So? What do you think?" I asked.

"I think she sounds like a complete psycho," Hannah said.

"My mom said pretty much the same thing," I said. "But even if that's true, there's nothing I can do about it, right? Charlie and Finn don't see her for what she is. And her short story has already been chosen for *The Ampersand*. It's not like I can undo that."

"That's the really sketchy part," Hannah said. "Well, no, I take that back. Everything she's doing sounds sketchy. But the short story is the part that doesn't make any sense."

"Sure it does. It's one more thing for her to copy from me. Remember how you noticed that Nora was dressing the same as me? She even bought exact duplicates of some of my clothes. Becoming a writer for *The Ampersand* was just the next step," I argued.

"No, that's not what I meant. Of course she submitted her story because she knew you wanted to get yours published. But the question is, Where did she get her story from?" Hannah asked. "Do you really think she just wrote it overnight?"

"It must have been something Nora had been working on," I said.

"That Nora never mentioned to you? Not once? Not even when you told her that you write?" Hannah asked. She raised her eyebrows, which had recently grown back after being waxed off for a photo shoot during her short-lived modeling career.

"Yeah, I know. It is strange," I said.

"It's more than strange. It's downright fishy," Hannah said.

It slowly dawned on me what Hannah was saying.

"Wait. You don't think she wrote that story herself?" I asked.

"Do you?" Hannah asked.

"I just assumed she had. I mean, submitting a story for publication that you didn't write . . . That would be really bad. And where would she have gotten it from?" I asked.

"I'm sure she copied it from somewhere," Hannah said, shrugging.

"But that's plagiarism," I said. "She could be kicked out of school for that. She wouldn't take that kind of risk. Would she?"

"From what you've told me, I wouldn't put anything past her. You know, maybe it's a good thing Dex is away at school. She'd probably have swooped in on him, too," Hannah said.

"Actually, Nora's specifically mentioned how much she's looking forward to meeting Dex when he's home for Thanksgiving break," I said.

"See?" Hannah shuddered. "Incredibly creepy. It's almost like having a stalker."

"But no one's going to believe me," I said. "She has both Charlie and Finn fooled. And *The Ampersand* editor, too."

Hannah sat up straight. "You'll just have to prove it," she said. "Prove that the story isn't hers."

"How can I do that?" I said. "First of all, I haven't even read her story. And second, I'm sure that if she is passing a published short story off as her own, she wouldn't have been dumb enough to pick a well-known one."

"There must be a way to research it. Couldn't you get a computer program to do that for you?" Hannah asked.

"Probably. But I wouldn't know how to create a program that would do that," I said. Computers had never been my thing.

"Finn could do it," Hannah said.

"Sure, he could. But I don't know if he would. He likes Nora. And he thinks I'm jealous of her," I said.

"How annoying," Hannah said. "Maybe Emmett could help. I'll ask him."

"That would be great," I said. I hesitated, and then smiled for the first time since the disastrous *Ampersand* meeting. "Thanks, Hannah."

"For what?"

"For listening to me. And for believing me," I said.

Hannah smiled back at me. "That's what sisters are for," she said.

•

Charlie called after dinner. Willow and I were out for our evening walk down the beach.

"Nora told me what happened," she said.

I wondered whether Nora had called Finn, too. Probably. She was rallying my friends to her side.

"Oh yeah?" I said. I tried to keep my voice as neutral as possible, but vented my frustrations by kicking a broken fragment of shell out of my path. Willow started at the sudden movement, and then looked up at me reproachfully.

"She said you seemed really mad," Charlie continued.

"I have no interest in hearing anything she said," I said.

"So you *are* mad."

"Charlie, I really don't think you should get in the middle of this," I said.

"I don't want to be in the middle. But Nora called me in tears. She's really upset," Charlie said. "I think you should talk to her. I know she wants to talk to you."

"That's funny, considering she hasn't called me," I said. I'd lost the battle to remain calm. Anger leaked into my voice.

"She thinks that if she does, you won't talk to her. Or that it will somehow make things worse between you," Charlie explained.

"Did she tell you what she did?"

Charlie sighed. "She told me that her story was selected to be in *The Ampersand*."

"And you think that what she did was okay?" I asked.

"I absolutely think she should have been up front with you about her intentions to submit her story," Charlie said. "But . . ."

I gritted my teeth. "But?" I said.

"But I think she had every right to have her story considered," Charlie admitted.

"I knew you would take her side," I said. The words tasted bitter on my tongue.

"I'm not taking her side! I'm not taking sides at all," Charlie said.

"Of course you are. You just called to tell me I should talk to her. That's taking a side," I said. Willow pulled at her leash, wanting to get closer to a trio of seagulls that was strutting around on the wet sand. I gave her a gentle tug back, and wound the leash around the hand I wasn't using to hold my phone.

"It's taking a side to encourage you to work out a problem with a friend?" Charlie asked.

"Nora is *not* my friend," I said flatly.

"Just because her story was selected over yours?" Charlie asked.

I felt as if I'd been sucker punched. "Is that what you think?" I asked.

"What am I supposed to think? You've been jealous of Tabitha Stone ever since her book was published," Charlie said.

I couldn't help myself. "Self-published."

"Whatever. Then you were jealous of Tabitha when she got the fiction spot in the first issue of *The Ampersand*. And you were thrilled when she lost it. And now Nora has it, and you suddenly hate her," Charlie said. I could tell she was building an argument, much as a lawyer would. "And Finn told me that the other night when you were at Grounded, you were complaining about Nora. That you had some paranoid theory that she changes the way she acts around different people. Which is ridiculous."

"Ridiculous," I repeated. For the second time that day, I went cold all over. It felt like my body had been dipped in ice water.

"Yes, it's ridiculous. Nora's the same person whether she's with you or me or Finn or anyone," Charlie said. She sighed again. "Miranda, don't you think that you might be a little jealous of Nora, and you're letting that color the way you see her?"

I couldn't speak. There was no point telling Charlie how wrong she was, or explaining how manipulative Nora had been. No matter what I said, Charlie would just turn it around and say that I was jealous.

And, okay, sure, maybe I'd had a problem reining in my jealousy in the past. Maybe I was jealous that Tabitha Stone was always singled out for her writing ability. And maybe I had worried too much that Dex's ex-girlfriend was trying to get back together with him over the summer, or that he'd end up liking one of the girls in his study group. But this situation with Nora was completely different.

"I'm sorry you feel that way," I finally said, my voice an emotional croak. It was hard to get the words out past the lump in my throat. "Look, I have to go."

"Miranda, don't go. We should talk about this," Charlie said.

"No, thanks," I said. "I don't feel like talking anymore."

I ended the call, and stuck my cell phone back in my pocket.

Chapter Twenty-four

The next day, I got to school early and headed straight for *The Ampersand* office. Today, I was glad to find the office empty. It would make my job much easier. I got out the file where the completed articles were kept and paged through it. Nora's short story—titled "Lamp Light"—was near the top of the stack. I made a copy of the story and then put the original back in the folder. Five minutes after I'd first entered the office, I left with a copy of "Lamp Light" tucked in my backpack.

I haven't done anything wrong, I told myself. After all, I was on the magazine staff. I had every right to read the articles. In fact, Candace encouraged us to do so, so we could give the authors feedback. But, at the same time, I didn't want anyone—especially Nora—to know what I was up to. Probably because I had no intention of giving her constructive feedback. To the contrary, I was planning on using it to bust her.

The more I thought about Hannah's reaction, the more I thought she was right. What were the chances that Nora, who had never once expressed any interest in writing, just happened to have a short story on hand, ready to submit? Much less one that was good enough to blow Candace away?

I was dreading the morning ahead of me. Nora was in my lit class, and both Nora and Charlie were in physics. I didn't particularly want to talk to either of them. Especially not until I'd had a chance to investigate whether "Lamp Light" was an original work of Nora's.

Luckily, Nora was already there, sitting in her usual seat, when I arrived at Mrs. Gordon's room. I sat across the room from her. It meant having to sit next to Tabitha Stone, but that was vastly preferable to sitting next to Nora. Besides, Tabitha seemed much more quiet and withdrawn than usual, and her eyes looked suspiciously red.

"Hey, Tabitha," I said as I took the seat next to her.

She glanced up at me, startled. "Oh. Hi, Miranda," she said. I thought she looked a bit wary, as though worried that I would say something unkind to her about the lost fiction assignment. Guilt flooded over me. Why had I been so happy to hear she'd failed? Sure, Tabitha could be cocky, but that didn't mean I should take pleasure in her unhappiness. It really wasn't very nice.

I hesitated. "I'm sorry about your short story getting pulled," I said.

Tabitha shrugged and looked glum. "I really liked my story. I don't understand why Candace hated it so much," she said.

"I'm sure she didn't hate it," I said.

"No, she did. She actually said, 'I hated your story,'" Tabitha said.

"Really? That's harsh," I said. "But it's just her opinion. You never know why one person likes a story, and another doesn't."

"*Hates* it," Tabitha clarified.

"You know my mom's a writer, right?"

"Yes. She writes romances, right?" Tabitha said. To her credit, she managed not to sound snotty, even though I knew she probably considered commercial genre romances to be beneath her literary tastes.

"Yes," I said. "And Sadie always says that she ignores the reviews, both good and bad, because you're never going to make everyone happy all of the time."

"That's smart," Tabitha said, nodding slowly.

"And if it makes you feel any better, my piece got spiked, too," I said.

"It did? Why?"

I nodded. "It was my own fault. I interviewed my boyfriend for a piece on student athletes, and didn't disclose that I have a personal relationship with him. I didn't know I had to."

"Really? Well. That's not *so* bad," Tabitha said.

I smiled. I could tell that she didn't approve, but was making an effort to be nice.

"No, I screwed up. I should have known better," I said. "I understand why Candace pulled the piece."

"The thing that worries me is, what happens now? Will she ever give me another chance?" Tabitha asked.

"I know what you mean. I'm worried about that, too," I admitted.

Tabitha and I smiled shyly at each other. I realized that this was the first time I'd ever really talked to her without feeling consumed with jealousy. It made for a nice change. Tabitha and I might never be close friends, but there was no reason we couldn't be friendly.

Mrs. Gordon came in then, just as the bell rang. Her hair was, as usual, falling out of its sloppy bun, and as soon as she walked in the door, half of the papers she'd been carrying dropped to the floor.

"Oh, dear," Mrs. Gordon said.

"I'll get them for you," Sanjiv said, bounding over to help her pick them up.

"Thank you, dear. It's the homework you all did on the themes that arise in *Tom Sawyer*. Everyone did a wonderful job. If you wouldn't mind handing them out, Sanjiv, I'd appreciate it," Mrs. Gordon said brightly. "And we'll get started on today's topic, which is to discuss how Tom's character evolves over the course of the book."

Since the desks in Mrs. Gordon's classroom were arranged in a circle, Nora and I were in full view of each other, and even though I did my best to avoid meeting her gaze—I busied myself getting my laptop out, and then began to studiously take notes—I could feel her eyes on me. Finally I gave in and glanced in Nora's direction. She gave me a half smile and raised one hand in a meek wave. I raised my chin and looked coldly away.

Nora had messed with the wrong geek.

*

Charlie was harder to avoid. Our lockers were side by side, and we always sat together in the classes we had together. But I managed to avoid her until physics class. I considered moving to a different table and hoping that Mr. Forrester wouldn't notice, but then I decided that would be childish. And besides, Nora would probably just end up taking my vacated seat, and I didn't want to give her the satisfaction. So I sat down in my usual seat.

"Hey," Charlie said, plopping down next to me.

"Hi," I said.

"Are you still not talking to me?" Charlie asked, pulling out her physics book and setting it on the table with a thud.

I glanced sideways to the right. Nora wasn't there yet.

"I'm not not talking to you," I said.

"You hung up on me yesterday," Charlie pointed out.

"You weren't being particularly supportive," I said. "At least, not to me."

"That's not true. I do support you," Charlie said.

I turned to look at her, my eyebrows arching. "Really? Because that's not what it sounded like to me last night. It sounded like you were totally on Nora's side, and wouldn't even listen to what I was trying to say."

Charlie sighed. "I just thought it would help if you heard another perspective," she said.

"I didn't need perspective. I needed a friend," I said.

Before Charlie could reply to this, Finn arrived, looking grumpy. Even his Mohawk seemed extra prickly, sticking up in overly gelled spikes.

"Holla back, girlfriends," Finn said with an edge to his voice, by way of greeting. Then he slammed his books down on his desk and slumped down in his seat.

"Hey," Charlie and I said in unison.

"Why are you so grumpy today?" I asked.

Finn shrugged and kicked one sneaker against the leg of the table. Finally, he said, "I found out last night that Phoebe's dating someone else. Some football player at Orange Cove High."

Charlie's smile died. I could tell the news that Finn was feeling jealous over Phoebe's new boyfriend didn't make her overjoyed.

"I'm sorry, Finn. That's a really tough thing to find out," I said. "So I guess that means there's no chance you'll be getting back together, huh?"

"What? I don't want to get back together with her," Finn said with surprise.

"You don't?" Charlie asked.

"Then why are you so upset?" I asked.

"Because it means that she won the breakup. She got a new boyfriend before I got a new girlfriend," Finn said.

"It's not a contest," Charlie said.

"Yes, it is. It's totally a contest. And I lost," Finn said. "I hate losing."

"Hey, guys," a voice said from behind me. I looked up to see Nora standing there. She was smiling nervously and shifting from foot to foot. "What are you all talking about?"

I turned back around, ignoring her.

Charlie looked worriedly from me to Nora and back again, and said, "Hey, Nora."

Only Finn seemed oblivious to the tension between Nora and me. "We're discussing the best strategy for how to beat my ex in the breakup wars."

"Nora should be able to help you out with that. She just went through a breakup, too. Right, Nora?" I said, still not looking at her.

After an awkward pause, Nora said, "That's right. But my exboyfriend and I aren't at war. Our breakup was all very . . . mutual."

"How convenient," I said.

"Miranda!" Charlie said. "Look, can't you guys just—"

But before she could finish, the bell rang. Mr. Forrester, who had been sitting behind his desk, stood and said, "Come on, everyone. You know the rules. When the bell rings, you're to be in your seats, ready to get started. Nora, please sit down. Now."

Nora had no choice. She took her seat at the table next to ours. Charlie gave me an exasperated look, but I ignored it. Nora was bad news. And sooner or later, Charlie would figure that out.

Chapter Twenty-five

Emmett, Hannah, and I sat around the kitchen table at the beach house, each of us with a laptop and a copy of "Lamp Light" in front of us. I'd made duplicates of the short story on my way home after school.

"Nothing's coming up under the title 'Lamp Light,' " Hannah said. "There's a Lamp Light company that the sell lamps—big surprise. And there's a Lamp Light Ministries. But no short stories with that name."

"I'm not surprised. Nora's not stupid. If she was going to plagiarize someone else's work, she'd definitely change the name," I said.

I'd read the short story during lunch. Wanting to avoid both Nora and Charlie, I grabbed a few sandwiches from the lunch room, wrapped them in a paper napkin, and hid out in my car, the pages of the short story propped up against Bumblebee's steering wheel.

I had to admit, the story was good. In fact, it was *so* good, it made me surer than ever that there was no way Nora had written it herself.

The story was about a man whose wife is leaving him. He sits in the living room of their apartment, under the light of a single lamp, and listens to the sounds of her packing up her things in the bedroom. And while he sits there, he thinks back over his life with her.

He remembers their first meeting, and the first time she slid her hand into his, and their wedding night. He thinks back to the first fight they'd had as newlyweds, and the moment when he first suspects that she no longer loves him. Each flashback was short, only a sentence or two, but altogether it was incredibly powerful.

"Come on," I said out loud when I was finished. "Who in their right mind could possibly think a high school student would be able to write this?"

But that was the problem with Geek High. All of the kids at my school were so gifted and talented, that the maturity of the piece would just be chalked up to genius. And it was also the problem with Nora Lee. For whatever reason, people seemed to instinctively trust her. No one would ever believe that such a shy, sweet girl was capable of plagiarizing someone else's short story.

No one except me, that was.

"Are you sure we're talking about the same girl?" Emmett asked, looking up from his laptop. "Nora's in my Latin class. She seems harmless. Maybe a little shy, but nice enough."

"Oh, no. Not you, too," I said.

"Men are notoriously bad judges of character," Hannah said.

"Hey!" Emmett said.

"It's true," Hannah said, patting his hand affectionately. "I should know. I'm a matchmaker. It's why so many guys end up dating pretty girls who are entirely wrong for them. They have no judgment. They see a pretty face, and boom, that's it. They don't bother to look any deeper than that."

"But I don't think Nora is pretty," Emmett protested.

"It doesn't matter. The point is that your entire gender can't be trusted with character judgments," Hannah said.

"That's not true. Dex is a great judge of character," I said. It *was* true. For example, when Hannah's friend Avery had been throwing herself at Dex, he had seen her for the vain, shallow, manipulative girl that she was. And a lot of guys wouldn't have bothered to look past my geek-girl label.

"Miranda's right. I'm sure some guys are that superficial. But not all of us are. Look at me. You're gorgeous, but that's not why I love you. I love you for who you are, not what you look like," Emmett said.

"That is so sweet," Hannah cooed.

Emmett laced his fingers through Hannah's and pulled her toward him. They began to kiss.

"No, really. Don't mind me. Just pretend I'm not even here," I said.

Emmett and Hannah broke apart and looked up.

"What's that?" Emmett asked. His eyes were dreamy and unfocused.

"Less smooching, more researching," I ordered. "Come on. I know that story must be here somewhere."

Over the next hour, our Internet searches turned up nothing. I'd even taken direct quotes from the story and Googled them, but no matter what I tried, nothing came up. Emmett went through the table of contents of various short-story anthologies on Amazon.com. Hannah continued to focus her attention on the title "Lamp Light," although I kept catching her covertly shopping on Net-a-Porter.com.

Finally, in frustration, I typed the phrase *short story about a man whose wife is leaving him* into the Google search engine, not expecting anything to come up. And, at first, the search results didn't seem promising. There was a link to an out-of-print Wilkie Collins novel written in the 1870s, a blog entry written by a guy who was going through a divorce, and a few e-zine articles with tips for saving a failing marriage. I scrolled through these, feeling increasingly gloomy about my chances of finding anything worthwhile, and wondering if I could have possibly been wrong after all.

Did Nora really write that amazing story? I wondered. Because if she had, then she had beaten me fair and square. My story was good and I was proud of it, but it couldn't compete with "Lamp Light." That was the sort of writing I hoped to eventually mature into someday. Maybe Nora truly was a gifted writer.

And, if so, maybe I'd been wrong about her all along.

But then I hit the jackpot.

It was another blog entry, and a short one at that. The name of the blog was A Dream within a Dream—which apparently was a reference to an Edgar Allan Poe poem—and the entry was dated two years earlier:

> Just read the most amazing short story called "One Afternoon" in this month's issue of *The New Yorker*. It's about a man whose wife is leaving him. He's sitting there, impotent to stop her, and thinking back on their life together and how much he loves her. It made me cry. I've never heard of the author before—someone named Enzo Lowry—but I'm definitely going to look for his future work.

I stood, staring at the blog entry, hardly able to believe it.

"Gotcha," I said.

"You found something?" Hannah asked. She'd looked up from her laptop, where she'd been browsing for shoes on Zappos for the past ten minutes.

"I think so," I said.

Hannah pulled her chair around next to mine, and Emmett got

up and stood behind us. With shaking fingers, I pulled up *The New Yorker* Web site, and typed in *One Afternoon* and *Enzo Lowry* into their search engine.

"'One Afternoon'? That's a stupid title. 'Lamp Light' is much better," Hannah said.

"Especially since there was so much imagery in the story about the lamp. How the bright light kept distracting him from his memories and bringing him into the present," Emmett said.

This time, what I wanted was at the very top of the search results:

"One Afternoon," Lowry, Enzo

I clicked on it, and started to read.

He sits in the green velvet chair that they bought together at the Twenty-sixth Street Flea Market, listening to her in the next room. The creak of the closet door. The dull thump as the suitcase is pulled down. The drawers sliding open.

"Oh, my gosh," I said.

"Is that it?" Hannah asked.

"That's it. Word for word, it's the same story," I said.

My heart thumping, I scrolled through the rest of the story to make sure that the trend continued. Sentence after sentence, page after page, "One Afternoon" was an exact duplicate of "Lamp Light." Or, more to the point, "Lamp Light" was an exact duplicate of "One Afternoon."

"I was right," I said, shaking my head. "I can't believe it. I was *right.*"

"Don't you mean *I* was right? This was my idea, after all," Hannah said.

"Yes. You were right. You totally nailed it," I amended.

"See? That's because I'm a good judge of character," Hannah said, tossing her hair back with a satisfied swish.

"And I guess I'm not, because I really didn't think we were going to find anything," Emmett said.

"That's okay, honey. You have other good qualities," Hannah said.

"Why would she take such a risk?" Emmett wondered. "I know *The Ampersand* is just a school magazine, but even so, it's pretty well-known. She had to know there was a chance someone would see the story and recognize it. Maybe even the author."

I opened up a new window and ran a Google search on Enzo Lowry.

"Here's his Wikipedia entry," I said, scanning over it. "It says he committed suicide in 2009. He was thirty-two."

"That's so sad. He was so young," Hannah said.

"And so incredibly talented," I added, continuing to read. "Apparently he wrote one book before he died, and it was a critical hit but hardly sold any copies. That's why he became suicidal."

"Nora probably thought she was safe copying from him," Emmett said.

"Now that I've found this, what do I do?" I asked.

"You bust her," Hannah said.

"Do you think I should confront her? Or go straight to Candace?" I asked.

"There's no point in confronting Nora. She knows what she did. She just didn't think she'd get caught," Hannah pointed out.

"That's true," I said. I hesitated. "But I'm not sure I want to go to Candace, either."

"Why not?" Hannah asked.

"She intimidates me," I admitted. "Plus, she knows that I wanted my short story to be published. If I'm the one who tells her about Nora, won't it look like sour grapes?"

"You could do it anonymously," Hannah suggested.

I shook my head. "Tempting, but no. That would be cowardly."

"Who's the faculty adviser for the magazine?" Emmett asked.

"Mrs. Gordon," I said.

"Tell her," Emmett suggested.

I nodded slowly. Mrs. Gordon was exactly the person I should talk to. She was kind and supportive and had always had an open-door policy with her students.

"I think you're right," I said. "I'll talk to Mrs. Gordon."

*

But before I talked to the faculty adviser, I decided to first talk to Dex. I sent him a text to see whether he was available. It took him a bit longer than usual to respond. While I waited, I used some of my nervous energy to clean up my desk, which looked like a bomb had exploded on it.

My cell phone chirped at me. I checked it, and there was a message from Dex saying he was online and ready to talk. I signed onto Skype and called him.

"Hey," Dex said. He smiled, but looked concerned. "Is everything okay? We weren't supposed to talk until after dinner."

"I know, I'm sorry. Is this a bad time?" I asked.

"Sort of. I was in a study group at the library," Dex said.

"Where are you now? Outside?" I asked. "I can see the trees behind you."

"Yeah, I'm sitting on a bench outside the library. Do you want to see the campus?" Dex asked. He turned his laptop slowly around, giving me a passing view of Brown Academy. It looked very pretty, with lots of rolling green spaces, leafy trees, and redbrick buildings covered in ivy.

"Very nice," I said, when he was back on camera again. "Do you want to go back to your study group? You can call me later."

"No, I'd much rather talk to you," Dex said, smiling at me. Even over the Internet, I could see the light in his eyes.

"Good. Because I need your advice on something," I said.

"I'll do my best," Dex said.

I filled Dex in on what I'd discovered about Nora that afternoon.

He whistled. "That's really bad," he said. "Couldn't she get kicked out of school for that?"

"Yep. Geek High has an honor code. If you violate it, you can be expelled. And plagiarizing would definitely be considered a serious violation," I said.

"I wonder why she did it. She had to know there was a risk she'd be caught," Dex said.

"I don't know. I guess she must have just really wanted the attention. Or maybe she just really wanted to beat me out," I said.

"But she didn't beat you. Not fair and square. How could she take any pleasure in winning if she knows she didn't deserve it?" Dex asked.

"Who knows?" I said, shrugging.

"So what part of this do you need advice on?"

I hesitated. "I was thinking I should tell the faculty adviser for *The Ampersand* about this. But if I do that, Nora's going to get in serious trouble."

"Sure she will," Dex said. "But that's not your fault. You didn't make her cheat."

"But the only reason I uncovered the fact that she did cheat was that I've been jealous of her. First, it felt like she was taking over my friends. Then she got her short story accepted over mine," I said.

"So what? You think you had impure motives?" Dex asked, looking skeptical.

"Well, didn't I?"

"No way. You had a gut instinct and you followed it. And you were right," Dex said.

"Do you think telling the faculty adviser is the right thing for me to do?" I asked.

"I think you have to. If you know the story has been plagiarized, you can't let *The Ampersand* go ahead and publish it. That would be unethical, too," Dex said.

"I hadn't thought of it that way," I said.

"That's what you have me for. Keeping you on the straight and narrow." Dex grinned mischievously.

I smiled back at him. "Thanks, Dex."

Chapter Twenty-six

Dex was right—knowing what I now knew, I did have an obligation to the magazine to make sure that Nora's plagiarized story wasn't published. *It's something I really should tell Mrs. Gordon in private*, I thought. Mrs. Gordon had told everyone on *The Ampersand* staff to feel free to call her at home if they ever had any questions or comments. So, feeling shaky with nerves at what I was about to do, I called her. Mrs. Gordon answered on the fifth ring.

"Hi, Mrs. Gordon. It's Miranda," I said.

"Hello, Miranda! To what do I owe this pleasure?" she asked.

"I have something I need to talk to you about in private. It's actually pretty important," I said.

"Can you come over now?" Mrs. Gordon asked.

Ten minutes later, I was in Bumblebee, driving over to the Gordons' house. Mr. and Mrs. Gordon lived in a small, one-story cottage on a quiet, sunny street near school. When I arrived, Mrs. Gordon was outside, planting impatiens in a pot on her front porch. When she saw me pull in, she smiled and waved, and then brushed her dirt-covered hands down the front of her jeans, leaving behind two muddy stripes.

"Hello, Miranda. Come on in. Can I get you a lemonade? I'm having one," Mrs. Gordon said as she led me into the house.

The Gordons' house was a lot like Mrs. Gordon—bright, cheerful, and endearingly sloppy. A pudgy yellow Labrador met us at the front door. After happily sniffing me and licking my hand, he followed us into the living room and settled in on a plump green dog bed, already covered in shed hair. Each of the living room walls was painted a different color—vivid pink, yellow, turquoise, Popsicle orange. The furniture was all shabby, but looked comfortable. Newspapers and magazines were stacked up on the coffee table, along with a jumble of incongruous items—a battered leather dog leash, a calendar that was two years out of date, what looked like a fishing lure. The clutter made the room seem even more homey.

It's the perfect place to curl up with a good book, I thought as I sat on a floral couch, sinking down into the cushions.

Mrs. Gordon returned with two sweating glasses of lemonade, handed me one, and then took a seat in a wing chair opposite me.

"Thank you for seeing me," I said.

"My door is always open," Mrs. Gordon said. "And I know you well enough, Miranda, to know that if you say something is important, it definitely needs my immediate attention."

These words of encouragement made me feel braver about what I was about to do. I took a deep breath and decided to blurt it out.

"I found out that Nora Lee plagiarized the story that she submitted to *The Ampersand*," I said.

The smile faded from Mrs. Gordon's face. "That's a very serious accusation," she said.

"I know," I said, nodding. "But it's true."

I handed her the story Nora had claimed to write and the original copy of "One Afternoon," which I'd printed off *The New Yorker* Web site. "'One Afternoon' was written by Enzo Lowry and was originally published in *The New Yorker* a few years ago. Nora's story, 'Lamp Light,' is an almost word-for-word copy of 'One Afternoon.'"

Mrs. Gordon put on a pair of reading glasses and began looking over the two stories I'd handed her. I sat quietly, not wanting to interrupt her. Finally, Mrs. Gordon put down the papers. As she read, her expression grew even grimmer. She took off her reading glasses and rubbed her temples, as though she had a headache.

"I'm sorry," I said, feeling guilty that I'd dropped this mess in her lap.

"Don't be. I'm glad you brought it to my attention. Can you imagine how much worse it would have been if we'd gone ahead and published it?" Mrs. Gordon said.

I nodded. "That's why I felt I had to tell you."

"Can I ask how you found out about this? Did Nora confess it to you? I know you and she are friends," Mrs. Gordon said.

"Actually, we aren't friends anymore. And, no, she didn't tell me. To be honest, I made a copy of her story without telling anyone, because I wanted to see whether it was better than the short story I submitted. I was jealous that Nora had beaten me," I said. Shame cut into me, deep and hot. But I felt that I had to admit to what I'd done.

Mrs. Gordon nodded. "And once you read it, you recognized it?"

"No. I just didn't think it seemed like something a teenage kid would write," I explained.

"Yes, I can see that. In fact, now that you point it out, it seems obvious," said Mrs. Gordon. "The protagonist is a middle-aged man going through a divorce. That's not a topic most high school students would choose to tackle."

"Plus, it was really, really good. Scarily good. It was written by someone who obviously put a lot of work into it. And that seemed odd to me, since Nora has never mentioned that she writes," I said.

"You had a gut feeling that all was not as it seemed," Mrs. Gordon said.

"Basically," I said. I hesitated. "What are you going to do?"

"This is a very serious matter. I'll meet with Headmaster Hughes first thing tomorrow to discuss it," Mrs. Gordon said.

"What will happen to Nora?" I asked.

Mrs. Gordon shook her head sadly. "That, I can't say. But, as you know, the school takes violations of the honor code very seriously. And this is one of the more serious honor code violations that I've come across in my entire teaching career."

I was surprised to discover that I was actually feeling sorry for Nora. Geek High was a small school, and news traveled quickly. By this time tomorrow, everyone would know that Nora Lee was a cheat. That wasn't going to be easy for her to live down.

I wouldn't tell anyone, I decided. Not even Finn and Charlie. They'd find out—everyone would find out, eventually—but I didn't want to be the one who started the rumor.

I stood. "Thanks again for seeing me," I said again.

"Anytime, Miranda," Mrs. Gordon said.

After dinner, I put Willow's leash on and led her toward the back deck. My dad was in the kitchen, putting dishes in the dishwasher.

"Are you going for a walk?" Dad asked.

I nodded.

"I'll come with you," he offered.

"Okay, sure," I said, even though I would have preferred to be alone. I needed to clear my head after all the drama of the day. But I didn't want to hurt my dad's feelings, so I waited while he loaded the last few dishes and then turned on the dishwasher. When he was finished, we headed out the back sliding-glass doors, onto the deck, and then down the long flight of wooden steps to the beach below.

It was still light out, although the sun was sinking in the sky.

The beach was largely deserted, except for a flock of small birds darting to and fro on the wet sand near the water's edge. The low, rhythmic rumble as the tide rolled in instantly calmed my rattled nerves. For the first time in hours, I was able to breathe deeply.

"You were very quiet at dinner tonight, Miranda," Dad said.

Dad, Peyton, Hannah, and I had eaten Chinese takeout. I'd been too busy drowning my sorrows in crisply fried egg rolls, kung pao chicken, and vegetable fried rice to say much of anything.

"Sorry. I didn't mean to be," I said.

"Rough day?" Dad asked.

"You can say that," I said. I told him about my discovery and subsequent meeting with Mrs. Gordon.

Dad whistled, which made Willow's ears prick up.

"That is tough. But it sounds like you handled it well," Dad said.

"I guess. Honestly, I sort of wish that I hadn't found out. That I wasn't the one who put it all in motion. I guess that makes me a big coward," I said.

"No, I think it's understandable why you would feel that way. But you have to remember, the easy option is rarely the best one," Dad said.

I smiled. "Dad's words of wisdom?" I asked.

"Hey, you should take what little I've got," Dad said.

Willow tugged on her leash as she bent forward to sniff at a discarded sandwich wrapper.

"Yuck. Litter," I said, picking it up and stuffing it in my pocket, to be thrown out later. Willow looked up at me, clearly perplexed as to why I'd taken it away from her.

"So what happens to Nora now?" Dad asked.

"I don't know. I asked Mrs. Gordon, but she wouldn't say. But I think Nora could be suspended or even expelled," I said. Even though it was still warm out, I felt a shiver run through me.

"You did the right thing, Miranda," Dad said.

"People keep telling me that," I said.

"And you don't believe it?"

"No, I do. I get that once I found out, I had to tell. I do. I just feel bad about it, that's all," I said.

Dad wrapped an arm around my shoulders and gave me a reassuring squeeze.

"How do you feel things are going at home?" he asked. "You and Peyton seem to be getting along better."

"We are," I said, nodding. It was true: Peyton had been a lot less hostile lately. She'd even stopped spontaneously suggesting all the various plastic surgery procedures she thought I could use. In fact, every time I thought she might be on the verge of insulting me, she'd suddenly stop, press her lips together, and walk away. It was definite progress.

"I think our family retreat really helped," Dad said, looking pleased with himself.

I glanced sideways at him. "Seriously?"

"Yes. It brought us all together. Made us all realize how important it is to stick together as a family," Dad said.

"Dad. We only lasted through an hour of that retreat. Then we fled," I reminded him.

"But that in itself brought us together. We made the decision to leave as a family," Dad said.

"No. Peyton, Hannah, and I made the decision to leave. You were hanging on the rope ladder, yelling for us to come back," I said. "Are you going to try to argue that that was your plan from the beginning? To get the three of us to bond together in order to bust out of that hideous camp?"

My dad grinned down at me. "Would you buy that?"

"No," I said, and we both laughed.

Chapter Twenty-seven

Nora wasn't in lit class the next morning, and Mrs. Gordon seemed more subdued than usual as she introduced our new book, *Last of the Mohicans*. I wondered where Nora was. Could she be meeting with Headmaster Hughes right at that very moment? Had she been suspended? There was no way to know, so I tried to focus on taking notes.

When I got to physics, Charlie said hello, but seemed otherwise aloof. Apparently, she hadn't forgiven what I'd said to Nora in class the day before. I tried not to let it bother me. I knew it was only a matter of time before Charlie found out that I'd been right all along about Nora.

Finn loped in, threw his backpack on the table, and then turned to face Charlie and me.

"Have you heard the news?" he asked.

"Are you growing a beard?" Charlie asked.

Finn ran a hand over his prickly chin. "Why, yes. Yes, I am. What do you think?"

Charlie shook her head. "Not a good look," she said.

"That's because it's in the awkward growing-out stage," Finn explained. "It'll look better when the full beard is in."

"Are you going to keep the Mohawk?" Charlie asked.

"Of course. It's my new signature look," Finn said.

"So you're going to have a Mohawk and a full beard," Charlie clarified.

"That's right, baby," Finn said.

"Bad, bad idea," Charlie said, shaking her head again.

"Miranda? Are you going to stick up for me?" Finn asked.

"What? Oh. About the beard?" I asked. "No. Not a good look."

"I get no support from my peeps," Finn complained. "How about a soul patch?"

"Ick," Charlie said.

"If you're going to insult this"—Finn waved a hand in front of his face—"I'm not going to tell you my grade-A gossip."

"Okay," Charlie said.

"Fine with me," I said, suspecting that I already knew what his gossip was.

"Okay, fine, stop badgering me. I'll tell you," Finn said. He leaned in close. "Nora was *expelled*."

It felt like someone had poured cold water down my back. So a decision had been made. And Nora had not fared well.

"What?" Charlie asked. "What are you talking about?"

"Nora was expelled," Finn repeated patiently.

"Nora who?" Charlie asked.

"Who do you think? Nora Lee. How many Noras do you know? It's not exactly a common name," Finn said.

Charlie gasped. "*Nora* was *expelled*? Why? What happened?" She turned to look at me. "Miranda, did you know about this?"

"I didn't know she had been expelled," I said.

"You know that short story she submitted to *The Ampersand*? The one that was going to be published?" Finn asked.

Charlie nodded and leaned forward, eager to hear more.

"She copied the entire thing from a short story that appeared in *The New Yorker*," Finn said.

There was no point asking Finn where he'd heard this from. Finn loved to gossip, and one of his favorite people to gossip with was Mrs. Boxer, secretary to Headmaster Hughes. He always got his best dirt from her.

Charlie's jaw dropped open.

"Are you *serious*? She was expelled?" Charlie asked.

Finn nodded. "That's the word on the street," he said.

Charlie turned to me, her mouth still hanging open. "Did you hear that?" she asked.

"Yeah," I said. "I heard."

Charlie frowned. "You don't look surprised."

"Of course I'm surprised," I said. "It's very surprising news."

Charlie continued to regard me suspiciously, but before she could question me further, the bell rang. As usual, Mr. Forrester stood and flapped his hands at us to be quiet. Obligingly, I turned to face the teacher, glad to escape the interrogation for now.

•

As I suspected, news of Nora's expulsion passed through the school at lightning speed. By lunchtime, it was the general topic of conversation buzzing through the corridors and the lunchroom. I kept hearing Nora's name, even though I was doing my best not to listen to what anyone was saying. Charlie kept shooting me suspicious looks, but didn't interrogate me further. I had a feeling she was holding back until she could corner me in private.

It was a relief to get into Bumblebee at the end of the day and drive myself home to the beach house. At least there I could get away from all of the Nora talk. But a half hour after I arrived home, there was a knock at my bedroom door. I was sitting on my bed, working on the lit homework.

Assuming it was Hannah, I called out, "You don't have to knock. Just come on in."

But it wasn't Hannah.

"Hey," Charlie said.

Charlie was dressed as a rocker girl, wearing dark skinny jeans, a black T-shirt, and a flowy, zebra-striped cardigan. On her feet, she wore red Converse sneakers.

"Hi. What are you doing here?" I asked, eyeing her warily. Charlie didn't normally stop by unannounced. I was pretty sure that her doing so today of all days meant that she had an agenda.

"So, what did you know, and when did you know it?" Charlie asked abruptly. She parked herself on the foot of my bed and stared at me, her head cocked to one side, which made her look like an inquisitive, green-haired bird.

I sighed and stretched my legs out in front of me.

"Hi, Charlie. Nice to see you, too. Me? I'm great. Thanks for asking," I said.

"I know you, Miranda. There's something you're not telling me," Charlie said.

"So? I don't have to tell you everything," I said crossly.

"We're supposed to be best friends," Charlie said.

"Funny, it hasn't seemed like it lately. You've been spending all of your time with Nora, and then jumping all over me just because I didn't buy her act. And, as it turned out, I was right," I couldn't help adding.

Charlie sighed and ruffled one hand through her hair. "Maybe I was wrong about Nora," she admitted.

"Maybe?" I said.

"Okay, I was wrong. I never thought she'd purposely undermine your getting your story published in *The Ampersand*," Charlie said.

"Thanks for acknowledging it," I said.

"Do you know how they found out she'd copied the story?" Charlie said.

I shrugged. "Maybe," I said.

"How?"

I puffed my cheeks and blew out a long, deep breath. But I knew the time had come to confess to my part.

"I'm the one who found out about it," I said.

"You did? How?" Charlie asked.

"I suspected that she didn't write it herself. It just didn't sound like her, or like something any teenager could write. So I did some computer research, helped by Hannah and Emmett, and I found the original story she'd copied," I said.

Charlie shook her green-topped head. "I really misjudged her. And you tried to tell me, Miranda. I should have listened to you."

"That's okay," I said.

"No, it's not. God, I was such a jerk. I can't believe I accused you of being jealous of Nora," Charlie said.

Hearing Charlie admit she was wrong didn't feel nearly as good as I thought it would.

"To be honest, I *was* jealous," I admitted. "I was jealous that her story got picked over mine, and I was jealous of her friendship with you."

"I'm sorry I made you feel that way," Charlie said.

I leaned back against the pile of pillows propped up against my headboard. "It's not your fault. It's something I have to work on. I can't go around feeling jealous all the time. It's no way to live."

"No," Charlie agreed. "There's always going to be someone out there who's smarter or prettier or more successful. If you focus on that too much, you'll go nuts. You have to be happy with who you are."

"Exactly," I said. I hesitated. "Have you talked to Nora?"

"No. I tried calling her, but she isn't answering her phone," Charlie said.

"In a weird way, I kind of feel sorry for her," I said.

"Really? Even after she cheated to beat you out?" Charlie asked.

"I know that wasn't a nice thing to do," I said.

Charlie snorted. "It was a horrible thing to do."

"But why did she feel like she needed to do it?" I asked. "Why did she want to beat me so badly that she'd actually risk copying someone else's work?"

Charlie hesitated. "She did something else, too," she said. "But I don't know if I should tell you."

"What?"

"It's just going to make you mad," Charlie warned.

"Now you have to tell me," I said.

Charlie played with the black rubber bracelets she wore stacked up on one wrist. "Nora told me that you told her you like Finn," she said.

"So? I do like Finn," I said.

"I mean *like him* like him. In a romantic way," Charlie explained.

"What?" I shrieked. "Are you serious?"

Charlie nodded. "At first she just hinted at it. She said things like, 'Are you *sure* there's nothing going on between Miranda and Finn?' And I kept saying, 'No way.' I mean, you're with Dex. And you've never had feelings for Finn, at least not that I know of."

"Never!" I said. "Never, ever, never!"

"Right. So that's what I told Nora. And she finally told me that you'd admitted to her that you liked Finn, but didn't want me to know about it. She said the whole reason you kept encouraging me to tell Finn how I feel about him it was because you were hoping it would backfire," Charlie said.

"That's ridiculous! I can't believe what a liar she is! Did she do the same thing with Finn? Tell him something so he'd be mad at me, too?" I demanded.

"Who knows? Finn probably wouldn't even notice if she did. You know how clueless he is," Charlie said.

"Even so. It's so underhanded," I muttered. "And you seriously believed her?"

Charlie smiled faintly. "Part of me knew she had to be making it up. Or, at the very least, had misunderstood something you'd said. But I have to admit, a small part of me couldn't help wondering if she was telling the truth, and if you weren't the friend I've always thought you were," she said. "I think that's part of the reason why I didn't take your side when you first told me your suspicions about Nora."

"When did you know she was lying?" I asked.

"Honestly? Just now when I saw your reaction," Charlie said.

"I've never had romantic feelings for Finn. And I never will," I said.

"I know. I mean, I know that now," Charlie said. She took a deep breath. "And I've decided that you're right. I do have to talk to Finn. I'm going to tell him how I feel."

"Seriously?" I asked.

"Seriously," Charlie said.

"Are you nervous?" I said.

"Of course. I'm terrified. But you know what? I have a feeling that the conversation is going to go okay. I saw the way Finn acted when he found out I'd gone out with Chad. And, yeah, I know that I shouldn't have done that just to make Finn jealous. But, even so, his response was encouraging. I think it's going to be good. Actually, I think it's going to be pretty great," Charlie said. A rosy flush was coloring her cheeks.

"Wow," I said. "This is a big deal."

"I know," Charlie said.

I wondered what would happen. Finn, Charlie, and I had been a trio ever since the seventh grade. If the two of them started dating—or if they started dating and then broke up—what would that do to our friendship? But I tried not to dwell on it too much. Things would happen as they happened. There was no way to predict how it would all unfold.

Chapter Twenty-eight

Over the next week, talk of Nora's plagiarism continued to swirl around Geek High. I got tired of hearing about it. Nora had been so quiet and shy, most people hadn't taken the time to get to know her. But everyone knew I'd been friends with Nora—and quite a few of them had also heard that she and I had had a falling-out even before her plagiarism was discovered. As a result, I was constantly peppered with questions about what Nora had been like, and had I suspected what she was up to. I shrugged most of these questions off. I didn't feel like talking about it.

Gradually, things in my own life got back to normal. Through Hannah, I found out about an Orange Cove High junior named Patrick Shaw. He was a nationally ranked junior tennis player, and was currently helping to organize a charity tennis tournament to raise funds for leukemia, which his little sister had been diagnosed with six months ago. I contacted Patrick, and he agreed to be interviewed for my student-athlete profile that would eventually appear in the second issue of *The Ampersand*.

Candace didn't accept my short story for publication in the first issue—after the plagiarism debacle, she decided to temporarily omit the fiction feature—but she told me she would absolutely consider my work for future issues, which was encouraging.

The most startling development happened after school one day. I was on my way out to the student parking lot when I saw Charlie and Finn standing near Charlie's old station wagon. They didn't notice me—they were talking so intently, I don't think they'd have noticed a full brass band marching by—and then, suddenly, Finn leaned over and *kissed Charlie*.

I promptly dropped my car keys. Luckily, Finn and Charlie didn't hear. The last thing I wanted to do was interrupt them. I scrambled for the keys and then hurried to my car before they noticed me.

"Oh, my gosh," I said under my breath. "Way to go, Charlie!"

I climbed into Bumblebee and drove home, smiling all the way. Charlie hadn't told me when she was planning to talk to Finn, or what she would say when she did, but obviously it had worked. And somehow, the idea of the two of them together didn't weird me out anymore. Even though they'd been friends forever, and even though they bickered constantly, something about the two of them together just seemed right.

As Hannah might say, it was a good match.

I pulled into the driveway of the beach house. My mind was still so full of thoughts of Charlie and Finn that at first I didn't see the girl sitting on my front doorstep, her shoulders slumped and her arms wrapped around her bent knees.

It was Nora.

All of my fizzy, happy thoughts instantly vanished.

What is she doing here? I wondered.

As I parked Bumblebee and climbed out, my pulse was humming. I couldn't tell if it was from anger or nerves, or a combination of both. Why would Nora come find me, of all people? I was the friend she'd betrayed. After all that she'd done, what could she possibly have to say to me?

Nora stood as I approached. She was wearing a black T-shirt over faded denim cut-offs and scuffed canvas sneakers. It was almost exactly what she'd been wearing the first time I laid eyes on her.

"Hi," Nora said. She stood with one arm down at her side, and the other crossed over her body.

"Hi," I said, stopping a few feet in front of her. "What are you doing here?"

"I wanted to talk to you," Nora said.

"What about?"

"Everything," she said. "Can I come in?"

I hesitated. I didn't want her in my life, and I certainly didn't want her in my house.

"Please," Nora said. "I won't stay long. I'll just say what I've come to say, and then I'll leave you alone."

Finally, I shrugged and gave a curt nod. *We might as well get this over with*, I thought. And I had to admit, I was curious to know what she would say.

As usual, Nora recoiled from Willow's exuberant greeting at the door. I'd once wondered why Nora disliked Willow, and why Willow was never as friendly to Nora as she was to our other guests. Now, in light of all that had happened, it seemed like it was an early warning sign I should have paid more attention to.

I petted Willow's head, and then said to Nora, "Let's go back to my room."

I led the way, Willow at my side, Nora trailing behind. Once we were there, I closed the door behind us. I was glad Hannah wasn't home from school yet. She'd have been dying to know why Nora was here, and would probably have eavesdropped at the door.

I dropped my backpack on my desk.

"Have a seat," I said, gesturing toward the desk chair.

Nora obediently sat down. I sat cross-legged on my bed, facing her, and waited.

"You probably hate me now, huh?" Nora said.

I didn't say anything. I just continued to look at her.

"I wouldn't blame you if you do. I know I deserve it," Nora said. "You were the first person who was nice to me at Geek High. And, in return, I was pretty awful to you."

"Yes, you were," I agreed.

Nora fell silent, staring at the floor in front of her. After just a few moments of this, I started to feel my patience slipping. If she'd come here for sympathy, or if she somehow thought we could be friends again, well, she was dead wrong on both counts.

"Nora, why did you come here? What did you want to say to me?" I finally asked.

She shrugged miserably. "I just wanted to apologize."

"Fine. Then apologize," I said.

"I'm really sorry, Miranda," she said.

I nodded. "Thanks, but I don't forgive you."

Nora nodded and bit her lip. "I sort of figured you wouldn't."

"I thought we were friends," I said.

"I thought so, too," Nora said.

"Then why did you do it? Why did you submit that story to Candace, when you knew how badly I was hoping to have my short story picked for publication? And why did you tell Charlie that I like Finn?" I asked.

Nora shrugged again. "I don't know, exactly. I think I was just jealous of you."

This took me by complete surprise.

"Jealous? Of me?" I said. "Why?"

"Because you have *everything*. You have friends and a cute boyfriend and a beautiful house. You're really smart, and everyone at school likes you. Everything's just so easy for you," Nora said. Her words came out in a burst, as though they'd been pent up inside of her for so long.

I just stared at her. I spent so much of my time being jealous of other people, it hadn't really occurred to me that someone would be jealous of me.

"Really?" I said.

"Yes, really. I don't have anyone. My parents don't even want me to live with them, and my grandmother barely tolerates my presence in her condo. No one wants me," Nora said. Tears were now leaking out of her eyes.

"It's not like my life is so perfect," I said. "My stepmother and I barely get along. And, yes, I have a great boyfriend, but he lives in a different state."

"So? At least you have a boyfriend! I've never even been on a date," Nora said.

"What about Marcus?" I asked.

Nora looked down at the floor, her cheeks flushing.

"I made him up," Nora admitted. "I was trying to impress you."

Aha! I thought. It was just as I had suspected.

"I didn't like you because you had a boyfriend. I liked you because you were fun to hang out with and nice. Or, at least, I thought you were," I couldn't help adding.

"I thought it would give us something to talk about. You know, if we both had long-distance relationships. I've always been really bad at talking to new people," Nora explained. She wiped at her cheeks with the back of her hands. I grabbed the tissue box off my nightstand and handed it to her.

"Thanks," Nora said. She took a tissue and dabbed at her eyes with it.

"I just don't understand why you turned on me," I said. "Did it make you feel better when you knew Charlie and I weren't getting along, or when the story you handed in got picked?"

"Actually, no. It made me feel sick to my stomach," Nora said.

"They why did you do it? How did it help you?" I asked.

"I don't know. I think I thought that if I could somehow step into your life and be just like you—have your friends and your clothes and everything else—that I'd be happy," Nora said. She shrugged helplessly and shook her head. "I know it doesn't make sense. And I'm not trying to make excuses for what I did." She looked up at me. "I really am sorry, Miranda. The worst thing about all of this—worse than everyone finding out that I cheated with that story, worse than getting expelled from school—is that for once in my life, I had a really good friend. And I messed it all up."

I could feel tears welling up in my eyes. I took a tissue and wiped at them.

"And I know that you don't accept my apology and that you can't forgive me. But I really am so, so sorry," Nora said.

I nodded. "Thanks, Nora. I appreciate that." I hesitated and took a deep breath. "And I do accept your apology."

"You do?"

I nodded. "Yep."

"But aren't you still angry at me?" Nora asked.

Actually, my anger had faded. Which wasn't to say that I was ready to trust Nora or to be her friend again. But I did think she was truly and honestly sorry for what she'd done. And I knew it couldn't have been easy for her to come apologize in person.

"Not as much as I was," I said, shrugging. "By the way, how did you get here?"

"I walked," Nora said.

"Do you want a ride home?" I asked.

"That would be great," Nora said. She gave me a watery smile. "Thanks, Miranda."

"No problem," I said, and for the first time since Nora had arrived, I smiled back at her.

Chapter Twenty-nine

I sat outside of Headmaster Hughes' office, waiting for my appointment to see him. Mrs. Boxer—who was the school secretary, but preferred to go by her official title of Executive Administrative Assistant to the Headmaster—was sitting at her desk, typing. Mrs. Boxer was a large woman, tall and broad shouldered, with gray hair that she wore in a beehive and eyebrows that had been plucked to thin lines. I could tell from the way she kept glancing over at me that she was bursting with curiosity as to why I was there.

Finally, she couldn't stand it any longer.

"Can I tell the Headmaster why you're here?" she asked. She had an unusually high-pitched, breathy voice.

I suppressed a smile. Mrs. Boxer loved to gossip. Anything I told her would go straight into the school's rumor pipeline.

"No, thanks. I'll tell him at our meeting," I said.

"Okay, dear," Mrs. Boxer said. Her fingers hovered over her keyboard, as though she were about to go back to work. But then she decided to take another stab at uncovering some good dirt. "It's terrible what happened with the Lee girl, don't you think?"

"Mmm," I said.

Mrs. Boxer tsk-tsked. "In all of my years at this school, I've never heard anything like it. Plagiarizing a published story and trying to pass it off as her own. It's simply shocking."

She waited for me to join in with her condemnations of Nora. When I remained silent, she pressed on.

"I gather that you and Nora Lee were friends. And that you had a falling-out," Mrs. Boxer said.

"You can't believe everything you hear," I said, smiling politely.

"Which part isn't true? The part about you being friends, or the part about the falling-out?" Mrs. Boxer asked, leaning forward eagerly in her chair.

Fortunately, I was saved from having to answer this. The wood-paneled door that led to the headmaster's office swung open, and Headmaster C. Philip Hughes stood there.

"Miss Bloom. Please come in," he said.

•

Headmaster Hughes was as bald as an egg, with dark eyes that gave the impression of missing nothing, thick eyebrows, and a square jaw with a cleft chin. When he smiled, it was a close-lipped grimace that pulled the outer corners of his mouth down instead of up. I'd always found this disconcerting, as it meant that even when he was pleased, he looked disapproving.

I followed him into his large office, with its enormous desk, book-lined shelves, and fussy, old-fashioned furniture. He waved me into one of the navy blue damask wing chairs before taking a seat behind his desk.

"What did you want to see me about, Miss Bloom?" the head-master asked.

"I want to talk to you about Nora Lee," I said.

If Headmaster Hughes was surprised, he didn't show it. He just nodded and waited for me to continue.

"I'd like you to reconsider your decision to expel her," I said.

This time, I thought there was a flicker of surprise in Headmaster Hughes' dark eyes. He regarded me for a long moment, tapping his bridged fingers together.

"It was my understanding that you were the one who discovered Miss Lee's plagiarism and brought it to Mrs. Gordon's attention," he finally said.

"That's right," I said.

"You must have understood when you did so that Miss Lee would face serious consequences. After all, what she did was a breach of the honor code," Headmaster Hughes said.

I nodded. "I knew there would be consequences. And there should be. But does her punishment have to be so harsh?"

"The Notting Hill Independent School for Gifted Children is a very special place. Coming here is a privilege. Because of that, we take our academic integrity very seriously," Headmaster Hughes said.

I drew in a deep breath. "But I've talked to Nora. She's really sorry for what she did. And I believe her. She's not a bad person. She only did what she did because she was new here and trying to fit in," I said.

"We have new students at Notting Hill every year. None has ever felt the need to plagiarize another author's work and attempt to have it published under her own name. If that story had been published in *The Ampersand*, it could have ruined the reputation of the magazine. A reputation that has been built over many years, through the hard work of many fine students," he said.

"But it wasn't published. So no real harm was done," I said.

"I disagree. Dishonesty always has consequences," the headmaster said, shaking his head.

But I wasn't ready to give up yet.

"I'm not saying she shouldn't be punished. But couldn't you just suspend her, instead of completely expelling her? You could even put her on probation," I said.

"Miss Bloom, this isn't a criminal case and you are not Miss Lee's attorney, bargaining for a lesser jail sentence. Miss Lee violated the honor code. The punishment for a severe violation such as this is expulsion," Headmaster Hughes said.

I hesitated. "You won't reconsider?"

He shook his head. "I'm afraid not."

I nodded and stood. I wasn't surprised. I knew going in that I didn't have much hope of convincing the headmaster to change his mind. But I felt like I had to at least try.

"Thank you for seeing me," I said. "I appreciate your time."

"Anytime, Miss Bloom. But before you go, may I ask you a question?" the headmaster said.

"Sure," I said.

"Am I correct in my understanding that you also submitted a short story to *The Ampersand*? And that Miss Lee's plagiarized short story was chosen over yours?" he asked.

"Yes," I said.

"But despite that, you decided to come plead Miss Lee's case to me?"

I nodded again.

"Why?" he asked simply.

"I don't know, exactly. I guess it's that I really believed Nora when she said she was sorry. And doesn't everyone deserve a second chance?" I asked.

The headmaster nodded slowly. "A noble sentiment. But, unfortunately, second chances aren't always possible."

"They should be," I said, shouldering my backpack.

◆

"What's this I hear about you meeting with the headmaster today?" Finn asked at lunch.

Charlie shot me a sharp glance. "You met with Headmaster Hughes?"

I looked up from the chicken salad sandwich I was trying to work up the nerve to eat.

"It didn't take long for that to get out," I said.

"I have my sources," Finn said.

"Mrs. Boxer," Charlie and I said together.

"She's not my only source," Finn said with mild indignation.

"How do you get her to tell you this stuff? Do you have something on her that you're holding over her head?" I asked.

"Mwa ha ha," Finn laughed evilly. He wiggled his eyebrows up and down. "I'll never tell."

"What's going on, Miranda?" Charlie asked.

"I asked Headmaster Hughes to reconsider his decision to expel Nora," I said.

Charlie's mouth actually dropped open. Considering she'd just taken a bite of her sandwich, this was not attractive. "What? But why? After everything she's done to you?"

"Actually, I didn't tell you, but she came to see me," I said. "She apologized."

"And you believed her?" Charlie asked skeptically, her eyebrows arching.

"Seriously, M. That chick has issues. You should steer clear," Finn said.

I dropped my sandwich back on the plate. Even though my stomach was growling, I still couldn't bring myself to eat Geek High chicken salad. I picked up a limp carrot stick and munched on it instead.

"Yes, I believed her. And no, we won't be friends again. But I feel bad for her. She's had a tough time of it. She doesn't get a lot of support at home," I said.

"That doesn't excuse what she did," Charlie said.

"No, it doesn't. But I think she deserves some compassion," I said.

"So what did Hughes say?" Charlie asked.

I shook my head. "He said he's not going to reconsider her expulsion," I said.

"I'm not surprised. The headmaster is pretty hard-core," Finn said. "The other day he made me turn my T-shirt inside out."

"Which T-shirt?" Charlie asked suspiciously.

"The one that says, 'Your Favorite Band Sucks,'" Finn said.

"I can't imagine why he found that offensive," I said.

Finn missed the sarcasm. "I know, right? He said that words that rhyme with *truck* and *duck* are not appropriate for school. And I said, 'How about *muck* or *buck*? Are those okay?' And then he threatened me with a detention."

"You are a twit," Charlie said, although with much more affection than she normally used when insulting Finn.

In return, he slung an arm around Charlie. I was still getting used to their casual shows of affection. Luckily, they weren't obnoxious about it, and rarely made me feel like a third wheel.

"Are you going to eat that sandwich, Miranda?" Finn asked, eyeing my plate.

"It's all yours," I said, pushing it across the table to him.

Finn took a bite. "This actually isn't bad for Geek High tuna."

"That's because it's chicken," I said.

Finn made a gagging sound and spit the sandwich out into a napkin.

Chapter Thirty

I didn't see Nora at all over the next month. I knew from Hannah that Nora had enrolled at Orange Cove High School. Hannah said that Nora kept to herself, although Hannah had heard that Nora was working on the school newspaper.

Then, in early October, I came home after a Tuesday afternoon *Ampersand* meeting to find a battered-looking ten-speed bike parked in the driveway, and Nora again sitting on our front step.

"Hi," I said. "Is that your bike?"

Nora nodded and stood. "I bought it at a garage sale. I got tired of walking everywhere."

I hesitated, wondering why she was here. I'd forgiven Nora and truly wasn't angry anymore. But I also didn't want to start hanging out with her again. I hoped she wasn't hoping for a reconciliation.

"So, what's up?" I asked cautiously.

"I just came by to let you know that I'm leaving," Nora said.

"Where are you going?"

"I'm moving back to Boston to live with my mom," Nora explained.

"What about her fiancé?" I asked.

Nora made a face. "They broke up. The wedding's been called

off. So I'm allowed to return home. For now, anyway. My mom's never without a guy for long," Nora said. She must have seen pity in my eyes. "Don't worry; it's fine. Maybe this time she'll stay single until I leave for college."

I nodded. I hoped so, for Nora's sake. "When are you leaving?" I asked.

"Tomorrow," Nora said. "I'm all packed and ready to go. My grandmother's thrilled to get her condo back to herself. She's throwing a bridge party to celebrate. Anyway, I didn't want to leave without saying good-bye."

"I'm glad. Good luck with everything."

"Thanks. You, too," Nora said. "And, Miranda?"

"Yeah?"

"For what it's worth, thank you for being such a good friend to me at the beginning of the year. I haven't had a lot of friends, so . . . well. I'm just sorry I blew it," Nora said.

I didn't know what to say. I knew what she meant, though. I thought Nora was someone I might have been good friends with, had our relationship not been so irreparably damaged.

"Bye, Miranda," Nora said.

"Bye, Nora."

Nora turned and walked over to her bike. She wheeled it around, mounted it, and then looked back over her shoulder at me. I raised a hand, and she waved back. I watched her as she biked down the driveway and turned into the street, until she was out of my view.

◆

"I was thinking, Thanksgiving break is only six weeks away," Dex said that night, as we talked on Skype.

"I know. I'm counting down the days," I said, hugging a pillow to my chest.

"Me, too. Then I come back here, have four weeks of school, and then I'll be home for three weeks at Christmas," Dex said.

"Wow, three whole weeks," I said. After so many months apart, three weeks sounded like a decadent amount of time.

"I know, I can't wait. Please tell me you're not going to London," Dex said. "I don't think I could handle the disappointment."

I grinned, thinking that maybe it wasn't so bad having a long-distance boyfriend, after all, especially if he was this excited to see me. Maybe absence really did make the heart grow fonder.

"No, I'm not. I was worried that Sadie would be disappointed when I told her I'm staying here for the holidays, but she was fine with it," I said. "And Hannah's really excited about our first Christmas together as a family," I said. And for the first time, the idea that the four of us—Dad, Peyton, Hannah, and me—were a family of sorts didn't feel completely artificial and forced. "She's making all sorts of plans. We're going to go up to Sea World one day. They have a whole holiday display with seals and polar bears and Santa."

"Sounds great. Can I tag along?" Dex asked.

"You have to ask?" I said.

"I can't wait to get away from here for a while," Dex confessed.

"I thought you'd started to like it there," I said.

"I do, most of the time. But I'm ready for a break. Especially from trig class, which is kicking my butt," Dex said.

The doorbell rang. Willow sat up on her bed, blinking sleepily and yawning. She'd never been much of a watchdog.

"Was that your doorbell?" Dex asked.

"Yep," I said.

"Do you have to go get it?"

"No, someone else will. Everyone's home," I said. "You're still having problems with your trig class?"

"Right now, I'll be lucky if I pass," Dex said darkly.

"Are you serious? I'll help. What are you working on now?" I asked.

"I don't want to think about it," Dex said. "I barely get to talk to you as it is. I don't want to spend what little time we have talking about trig."

There was a knock at my door.

"Miranda? Are you in there?" Hannah called through the door.

"I'm kind of busy right now," I called back.

"Since when did Hannah start knocking?" Dex asked. "She usually just bursts in."

"I don't know. It's a relatively new development," I said.

Hannah opened the door anyway. She was frowning.

"Can this wait?" I asked her. "I'm talking to Dex."

"It's your mom," Hannah said.

"My mom? What about her?" I asked.

"She's here," Hannah said.

Chapter Thirty-one

"Surprise!" Sadie said.

She was sitting in the living room, perched on a leather chair. Sadie looked great. Since she'd moved to London, she'd traded in her long hair and hippie skirts for a short, sleek bob and tailored suits. I thought she might have also lost a little bit of weight; her jaw seemed more defined, and her waist was slimmer.

Seated across from Sadie on a low white sofa were my dad and Peyton. They both seemed tense. Sadie had always had that effect on my dad, even when they were married, and Sadie and Peyton had never gotten along. Only Sadie looked relaxed, lounging in her chair, completely at ease. She had always loved surprising people.

"Mom!" I said, rushing over to her. She stood and enveloped me in a hug. I breathed in her familiar scent of perfume mingled with coffee.

"What are you doing here?" I asked her, finally stepping back.

"I came to surprise you," Sadie said.

"It worked," I said. "I'm definitely surprised!"

"And I have news," Sadie said.

Sadie twinkled in Dad and Peyton's direction, as if they were all in on whatever she was up to. But I could tell from their twin confused expressions that Dad and Peyton had no idea what Sadie was about to announce.

"If you'd told me you were coming for a visit, I would have been able to pick you up from the airport. I have a car now," I said proudly.

"That's just it. I'm not here for a visit," Sadie said.

"You're not?"

"Nope. That's my surprise. I'm moving back to Orange Cove!" Sadie announced.

•

"Honestly, I thought you'd be happier about this," Sadie said, later that evening. She and I were sitting in a booth at Go Fish, eating fried grouper sandwiches served with generous amounts of French fries and pineapple-laced coleslaw.

"I'm still trying to adjust to the news. You did sort of spring it on me," I said.

"But you'll be able to move home! Get out of the beach house and away from Peyton!" Sadie said. "I thought you hated living there. What is it with that woman and the color white? Everything's white. The walls, the furniture, even the cat. Frankly, it's a bit creepy."

"Peyton likes white," I said. "And I don't think Madonna can help what color she is."

"Who's Madonna?"

"The cat," I explained.

"Anyway, darling, aren't you thrilled? We'll be together again! Just the two of us back in our bachelorette pad. Won't it be wonderful?" Sadie enthused.

"Absolutely," I said, trying to sound enthusiastic.

But the truth was, I wasn't at all sure what to think. A little over a year ago, I'd been furious at Sadie when she took off for London and left me behind. Back then, I barely knew my dad and couldn't stand my stepmother and stepsister. But over the past year, a lot had changed. My dad and I had grown a lot closer. And Hannah had become one of my best friends. True, Peyton and I didn't have the best relationship in the world, but even that had gotten better over time.

And besides, I was still angry at Sadie. She'd deserted me. And now that she was back, she just assumed that everything would be the same as it was before she left. That I'd be perfectly happy moving back in with her. But I wasn't at all sure that's what I wanted to do.

"I was thinking that now that I'm back, we should make every Saturday night our bohemian night," Sadie was saying, waving her fork around with enthusiasm. "We'll throw big parties and invite all sorts of different people over, and have long, intellectual discussions about the important topics of the day. How does that sound?"

"Actually, Mom, I think we need to talk about this," I said.

"About the boho nights? Okay, fine, although I think it's a fabulous idea. We could even have theme nights. Art night, music night, interpretative dance night," Sadie said. "And since when did you start calling me Mom?"

"No, not about the party nights. I think we should talk about my living arrangements," I said.

"Why? You'll move back home with me, darling. That's where you belong," Sadie said. "Now. Should we order dessert? Because I know we shouldn't—I'm watching my weight—but I have to say, I've been dreaming about having a slice of authentic key lime pie for over a year."

Sadie waved down the waiter. When he came over, she twinkled up at him.

"One slice of your *fabulous* key lime pie, and two forks, please," she said. Then she looked back at me and said, "So, tell me all about the dashing young Dex. Is he coming home for Thanksgiving?"

That night, I took Willow for a walk on the beach. I didn't tell anyone I was going out. Ever since Sadie's surprise arrival, there'd been a weird vibe in the house. Hannah was in her room, talking on the phone, and Dad and Peyton were still sitting in the living room, having a low, murmured conversation. So Willow and I slipped through the house, unheard and unseen, and headed out through the back door.

The beach was deserted, although a full moon hung low in the sky, illuminating our way. Willow picked her way daintily across the sand, stopping only occasionally to smell something interesting that had washed up on the beach.

Even though I was caught up in my thoughts, I couldn't help noticing how beautiful the pale sand looked in the moonlight, and how dark and mysterious the water was at night.

What am I going to do? I wondered. Everyone seemed to just assume that now that Sadie was back, I'd move back in with her. My dad was sad but resigned, and Hannah had shut herself away in her room. Even Peyton seemed oddly subdued, and I would have thought she'd be overjoyed at the news that I was on my way out of the beach house. Then again, Peyton and I had been getting along a lot better in recent months. *Maybe we've finally gotten used to each other*, I thought. Gotten used to sharing a house; sharing a family.

Willow tugged on her leash as she bowed her head to nose at a patch of seaweed. I waited while she sniffed it over thoroughly before deciding that no, the seaweed was not hiding a bacon sandwich.

What would happen if I just told Sadie no? I wondered. If I told her I was going to stay at the beach house, and live there until I graduated from high school. Would she be upset? Would she fight me over it?

The moon was casting a golden reflection down on the water that rippled with each passing wave. The ocean always reminded me of Dex, even at night. I expected to turn around on the beach and see him there, his eyes glinting, his mouth quirked up in a smile. Steady, reliable Dex, the one person I could always count on.

Willow tugged again gently at her leash. She'd spotted something in the distance—a bird? A plastic bag?—and was eager to investigate it.

"Okay, girl. We'll go check it out," I told her.

As we set off to hunt whatever it was, I realized suddenly that I was wrong. Dex *wasn't* the only person I could count on. I had lots of people I counted on. Charlie. Hannah. Dad. Even Finn (although how much anyone could count on Finn for anything without having to bribe him first was open for debate).

And then there was me. I'd learned I could count on myself. I'd proven that to myself just this school year. After all, everything that could go wrong had gone wrong. My boyfriend had moved away. Someone I'd trusted had deliberately set out to hurt me. My best friends hadn't backed me up. My first article for *The Ampersand* had been a failure. I'd been plagued with feelings of jealousy and insecurity.

But even after going through all of that, I was still here. I was happy and whole and a stronger person than I'd been a few months ago. I was standing on my own two feet, moving forward, ready to face whatever it was that was ahead of me.

And if I can count on myself, I thought, *nothing I face in the future can be all that bad.* That was what being fearless meant.

"Bring it on," I said out loud. "Bring it on!"

Willow paused in her hunt to look up at me questioningly.

"It's okay, girl," I said, patting her head. "I'm just letting the future know I'm ready for anything."

Photo by Marie Langmore

Piper Banks lives in South Florida with her husband, son, and smelly pug dog. You can visit her Web site at www.piperbanks.com.